Merry Xmas 1909
To Emma
from
Alice P. E.

FORTY MINUTES LATE
AND OTHER STORIES

"HOLD HARD, MEN!" HE CRIED. "KEEP STILL—ALL OF YOU!"

FORTY MINUTES LATE

AND OTHER STORIES

BY

F. HOPKINSON SMITH

ILLUSTRATED

CHARLES SCRIBNER'S SONS
NEW YORK : : : : : : : : : : 1909

CONTENTS

ILLUSTRATIONS

FORTY MINUTES LATE AND
OTHER STORIES

FORTY MINUTES LATE

IT began to snow half an hour after the train started—a fine-grained, slanting, determined snow that forced its way between the bellows of the vestibules, and deposited itself in mounds of powdered salt all over the platforms and steps. Even the porter had caught some puffs on his depot coat with the red cape, and so had the conductor, from the way he thrashed his cap on the back of the seat in front of mine.

"Yes, gettin' worse," he said in answer to an inquiring lift of my eyebrows. "Everything will be balled up if this keeps on."

"Shall we make the connection at Bondville?" I was to lecture fifty miles from Bondville Junction, and had but half an hour lee-way.

If the man with the punch heard, he made no answer. The least said the soonest mended in crises like this. If we arrived on time every passenger would grab his bag and bolt out without thanking him or the road, or the engineer who took the full blast of the storm on his chest

3

and cheeks. If we missed the connection, any former hopeful word would only add another hot coal to everybody's anger.

I fell back on the porter.

"Yes' sir, she'll be layin' jes' 'cross de platform. She knows we're comin'. Sometimes she waits ten minutes—sometimes she don't; more times I seen her pullin' out while we was pullin' in."

Not very reassuring this. Only one statement was of value—the position of the connecting train when we rolled into Bondville.

I formulated a plan: The porter would take one bag, I the other—we would both stand on the lower step of the Pullman, then make a dash. If she was pulling out as we pulled in, a goatlike spring on my part might succeed; the bags being hurled after me to speed the animal's motion.

One hour later we took up our position.

"Dat's good!—Dar she is jes' movin' out: thank ye, sar. I got de bag—dis way!"

There came a jolt, a Saturday-afternoon slide across the ice-covered platform, an outstretched greasy hand held down from the step of the moving train, followed by the chug of a bag that missed my knees by a hand's breadth—and I was hauled on board.

4

The contrast between a warm, velvet-lined Pullman and a cane-seated car with both doors opened every ten minutes was anything but agreeable; but no discomfort should count when a lecturer is trying to make his connection. That is what he is paid for and that he must do at all hazards and at any cost, even to chartering a special train, the price devouring his fee.

Once in my seat an account of stock was taken—two bags, an umbrella, overcoat, two gum shoes (one off, one on), manuscript of lecture in bag, eye-glasses in outside pocket of waistcoat. This over, I spread myself upon the cane seat and took in the situation. It was four o'clock (the lecture was at eight); Sheffield was two hours away; this would give time to change my dress and get something to eat. The committee, moreover, were to meet me at the depot with a carriage and drive me to where I was "to spend the night and dine"—so the chairman's letter read. The suppressed smile on the second conductor's face when he punched my ticket and read the name of "Sheffield" sent my hand into my pocket in search of this same letter. Yes—there was no mistake about it,— "Our carriage," it read, "will meet you," etc., etc.

The confirmation brought with it a certain

thrill; not a carriage picked up out of the street, or a lumbering omnibus—a mere go-between from station to hotels—but "our carriage!" Nothing like these lecture associations, I thought, —nothing like these committees, for making strangers comfortable. That was why it was often a real pleasure to appear before them. This one would, no doubt, receive me in a big yellow and white Colonial club-house built by the women of the town (I know of a dozen just such structures), with dressing and lunch rooms, spacious lecture hall, and janitor in gray edged with black.

This thought called up my own responsibility in the matter; I was glad I had caught the train; it was a bad night to bring people out and then disappoint them, even if most of them did come in their own carriages. Then again, I had kept my word; none of my fault, of course, if I hadn't —but I had!—that was a source of satisfaction. Now that I thought of it, I had, in all my twenty years of lecturing, failed only twice to reach the platform. In one instance a bridge was washed away, and in the other my special train (the price I paid for that train still keeps me hot against the Trusts) ran into a snowdrift and stayed there until after midnight, instead of de-livering me on time, as agreed. I had arrived

6

late, of course, many times, gone without my supper often, and more than once had appeared without the proper habiliments—and I am particular about my dress coat and white waistcoat—but only twice had the gas been turned off and the people turned out. Another time I had—

"Sheffield! Shef-fie-l-d! All out for Shef-f-i-e-l-d!" yelled the conductor.

The two bags once more, the conductor helping me on with my overcoat, down the snow-blocked steps and out into the night.

"Step lively!—more'n an hour late now."

I looked about me. I was the only passenger. Not a light of any kind—not a building of any kind, sort, or description, except a box-car of a station set up on end, pitch dark inside and out, and shut tight. No carriage. No omnibus; nothing on runners; nothing on wheels. Only a dreary waste of white, roofed by a vast expanse of black.

"Is this Sheffield?" I gasped.

"Yes,—all there is here; the balance is two miles over the hills."

"The town?"

"Town?—no, the settlement;—ain't more's two dozen houses in it."

"They were to send a carriage and—"

7

"Yes—that's an old yarn—better foot it for short." Here he swung his lantern to the engineer craning his head from the cab of the locomotive, and sprang aboard. Then this fragment came whirling through the steam and smoke:—"There's a farmhouse somewhere's over the hill,—follow the fence and turn to—" the rest was lost in the roar of the on-speeding train.

I am no longer young. Furthermore, I hate to carry things—bags especially. One bag might be possible—a very small one; two bags, both big, are an insult.

I deposited the two outside the box-car, tried the doors, inserted my fingers under the sash of one window, looked at the chimney with a half-formed Santa Claus idea of scaling the roof and sliding down to some possible fireplace below; examined the wind-swept snow for carriage tracks, peered into the gloom, and, as a last resort, leaned up against the sheltered side of the box to think.

There was no question that if a vehicle of any kind had been sent to meet me it had long since departed; the trackless roadway showed that. It was equally evident that if one was coming, I had better meet it on the way than stay where I was and freeze to death. The fence was still

visible—the near end—and there was a farmhouse somewhere—so the conductor had said,
and he seemed to be an honest, truthful man.
Whether to right or left of the invisible road,
the noise of the train and the howl of the wind
had prevented my knowing—but *somewhere's*—
That was a consolation.

The bags were the most serious obstacles. If
I carried one in each hand the umbrella would
have to be cachéd, for some future relief expe-
dition to find in the spring.

There *was* a way, of course, to carry bags—
any number of bags. All that was needed was
a leather strap with a buckle at each end; I had
helped to hang half a dozen bags across the shoulders of as many porters meeting trains all over
Europe. Of course, I didn't wear leather straps.
Suspenders were my stronghold. They might!—
No, it was too cold to get at them in that wind.
And if I did they were of the springy, wabbly
kind that would seesaw the load from my hips
to my calves.

The only thing was to press on. Some one
had blundered, of course.

"Half a league, half a league—into the
jaws," etc.

"Theirs not to reason why—"
But my duty was plain; the audience were

9

already assembling; the early ones in their seats by this time.

Then an inspiration surged through me. Why not slip the umbrella through the handle of one bag, as Pat carries his shillalah and bundle of duds, and grab the other in my free hand! " Our carriage" couldn't be far off. The exercise would keep my blood active and my feet from freezing, and as to the road, was there not the fence, its top rail making rabbit jumps above the drifts?

So I trudged on, stumbling into holes, flopping into treacherous ruts, halting in the steeper places to catch my breath, till I reached the top of the hill. There I halted—stopped short, in fact: the fence had given out! In its place was a treacherous line of bushes that faded into a delusive clump of trees. Beyond, and on both sides, stretched a great white silence—still as death.

Another council of war. I could retrace my steps, smash in the windows of the station, and camp for the night, taking my chances of stopping some east-bound train as it whizzed past, with a match and my necktie—or I could stumble on, perhaps in a circle, and be found in the morning by the early milk.

On! On once more—maybe the clump of trees hid something—maybe—

Here a light flashed—a mere speck of a light —not to the right, where lay the clump of trees—but to my left; then a faint wave of warm color rose from a chimney and curled over a low roof buried in snow. Again the light flashed—this time through a window with four panes of glass—each one a beacon to a storm-tossed mariner!

On once more—into a low hollow—up a steep slope—slipping, falling, shoving the hand-gripped bag ahead of me to help my footing, until I reached a snow-choked porch and a closed door.

Here I knocked.

For some seconds there was no sound; then came a heavy tread, and a man in overalls threw wide the door.

"Well, what do you want at this time of night?" (Time of night, and it but seven-thirty!)

"I'm the lecturer," I panted.

"Oh, come! Ain't they sent for ye? Here, I'll take 'em. Walk in and welcome. You look beat out. Well—well—wife and I was won-derin' why nothin' driv past for the six-ten. We knowed you was comin'. Then agin, the station master's sick, and I 'spose ye couldn't warm up none. And they ain't sent for ye? And they let ye tramp all— Well—well!"

I did not answer. I hadn't breath enough left for sustained conversation; moreover, there was a red-hot stove ahead of me, and a rocking-chair,—comforts I had never expected to see again—and there was a pine table—oh, a lovely pine table, with a most exquisite white oil-cloth cover, holding the most beautiful kerosene lamp with a piece of glorious red flannel floating in its amber fluid; and in the corner—a wife—a sweet-faced, angelic-looking young wife, with a baby in her arms too beautiful for words—must have been!

I dropped into the chair, spread my fingers to the stove and looked around—warmth—rest—peace—comfort—companionship—all in a minute!

"No, they didn't send anything," I wheezed when my breath came. "The conductor told me I should find the farmhouse over the hill—and—"

"Yes, that's so; it's back a piece, you must have missed it."

"Yes—I must have missed it," I continued in a dazed way.

"The folks at the farmhouse is goin' to hear ye speak, so they told me. Must be startin' now."

"Would you please let them know I am here, and—"

"YER AIN'T THE FUST ONE THEY'VE LEFT DOWN HERE TO GIT
UP THE BEST WAY THEY COULD."

"Sure! Wait till I get on my boots! Hello! — that's him now."

Again the door swung wide. This time it let in a fur overcoat, coon-skin cap, two gray yarn mittens, a pair of raw-beefsteak cheeks and a voice like a fog-horn.

"Didn't send for ye? Wall, I'll be gol-durned! And yer had to fut it? Well, don' that beat all. And yer ain't the fust one they've left down here to get up the best way they could. Last winter—Jan'ry, warn't it, Bill?" Bill nodded—"there come a woman from New York and they dumped her out jes' same as you. I happened to come along in time, as luck would have it—I was haulin' a load of timber on my bob-sled—and there warn't nothin' else, so I took her up to the village. She got in late, of course, but they was a-waitin' for her. I really wasn't goin' to hear you speak to-night—we git so much of that sort of thing since the old man who left the money to pay you fellers for talkin' died—been goin' on ten years now—but I'll take yer 'long with me, and glad to. But yer oughter have somethin' warmer'n what yer got on. Wind's kinder nippy down here, but it ain't nothin' to the way it bites up on the ridge."

This same thought had passed through my

13

own mind. The unusual exertion had started every pore in my body; the red-hot stove had put on the finishing touches and I was in a Russian bath. To face that wind meant all sorts of calamities.

The Madonna-like wife with the cherub in her arms rose to her feet.

"Would you mind wearing my fur tippet?" she said in her soft voice; "'tain't much, but it 'ud keep out the cold from yer neck and maybe this shawl'd help some, if I tied it round your shoulders. Father got his death ridin' to the village when he was overhet."

She put them on with her own hands, bless her kind heart! her husband holding the baby; then she followed me out into the cold and helped draw the horse-blanket over my knees; the man in the coon-skin cap lugging the bags and the umbrella.

I looked at my watch. After eight o'clock, and two miles to drive!

"Oh, I'll git yer there," came a voice from inside the fur overcoat. "Darter wanted to go, but I said 'twarn't no night to go nowhars. Got to see a man who owes me some money, or I'd stay home myself. Git up, Joe."

It was marvellous, the intelligence of this man. More than marvellous when my again blinded

14

eyes—the red flannel in the lamp helped—
began to take in the landscape. Fences were
evidently of no use to him; clumps of trees
didn't count. If he had a compass anywhere
about his clothes, he never once consulted it.
Drove right on—across trackless Siberian
steppes; by the side of endless glaciers, and
through primeval forests, his voice keeping up its
volume of sound, as he laid bare for me the
scandals of the village—particularly the fight
going on between the two churches—one hard
and one soft—this lecture course being one of
the bones of contention.

I saved my voice and kept quiet. If a run-
ner did not give out or " Joe " break a leg, we
would reach the hall in time ; half an hour late,
perhaps—but in time; the man beside me had
said so—and the man beside me knew.

With a turn of the fence—a new one had
thrust its hands out of a drift—a big building—
big in the white waste—loomed up. My companion flapped the reins the whole length of
Joe's back.

"Git up! No, by gosh!—they ain't tired
yet;—they're still a-waitin'. See them lights
—that's the hall."

I gave a sigh of relief. The ambitious young
man with one ear open for stellar voices, and the

15

overburdened John Bunyan, and any number of other short-winded pedestrians, could no longer monopolize the upward and onward literature of our own or former times. I too had arrived.

Another jerk to the right—a trot up an incline, and we stopped at a steep flight of steps— a regular Jacob's-ladder flight—leading to a corridor dimly lighted by the flare of a single gas jet. Up this I stumbled, lugging the bags once more, my whole mind bent on reaching the platform at the earliest possible moment—a curious mental attitude, I am aware, for a man who had eaten nothing since noon, was still wet and shivering inside, and half frozen outside— nose, cheeks, and fingers—from a wind that cut like a circular saw.

As I landed the last bag on the top step—the fog-horn couldn't leave his horse—I became conscious of the movements of a short, rotund, shad-shaped gentleman in immaculate white waistcoat, stiff choker and wide expanse of shirt front. He was approaching me from the door of the lecture hall in which sat the audience; then a clammy hand was thrust out—and a thin voice trickled this sentence:

"You're considerable late sir—our people have been in their—"

"I am *what!*" I cried, straightening up.

16

SHE PUT THEM ON WITH HER OWN HANDS.

"I said you were forty minutes late, sir. We expect our lecturers to be on —"

That was the fulminate that exploded the bomb. Up to now I had held myself in hand. I was carrying, I knew, 194 pounds of steam, and I also knew that one shovel more of coal would send the entire boiler into space, but through it all I had kept my hand on the safety-valve. It might have been the white waistcoat or the way the curved white collar cupped his billiard-ball of a chin, or it might have been the slight frown about his eyebrows, or the patronizing smile that drifted over his freshly laundered face; or it might have been the deprecating gesture with which he consulted his watch: whatever it was, out went the boiler.

"LATE! Are you the man that's running this lecture course?"

"Well, sir, I have the management of it."

"You have, have you? Then permit me to tell you right here, my friend, that you ought to sublet the contract to a five-year-old boy. You let me get out in the cold—send no conveyance as you agreed—"

"We sent our wagon, sir, to the station. You could have gone in and warmed yourself, and if it had not arrived you could have telephoned—the station is always warm."

17

"You have the impudence to tell me that I don't know whether a station is closed or not, and that I can't see a wagon when it is hauled up alongside a depot?"

The clammy hands went up in protest: "If you will listen, sir, I will—"

"No, sir, I will listen to nothing," and I forged ahead into a small room where five or six belated people were hanging up their coats and hats.

But the Immaculate still persisted:

"This is not where— Will you come into the dressing-room, sir? We have a nice warm room for the lecturers on the other side of the—"

"No—sir; I won't go another step, except on to that platform, and I'm not very anxious now to get there—not until I put something inside of me—" (here I unstrapped my bag) "to save me from an attack of pneumonia." (I had my flask out now and the cup filled to the brim.) "When I think of how hard I worked to get here and how little you—" (and down it went at one gulp).

The expression of disgust that wrinkled the placid face of the Immaculate as the half-empty flask went back to its place, was pathetic—but I wouldn't have given him a drop to have saved his life.

I turned on him again.

"Do you think it would be possible to get a vehicle of any kind to take me where I am to sleep?"

"I think so, sir." His self-control was admirable.

"Well, will you please do it?"

"A sleigh has already been ordered, sir." This came through tightly closed lips.

"All right. Now down which aisle is the entrance to the platform?"

"This way, sir." The highest glacier on Mont Blanc couldn't have been colder or more impassive.

Just here a calming thought wedged itself into my brain-storm. These patient, long-suffering people were not to blame; many of them had come several miles through the storm to hear me speak and were entitled to the best that was in me. To vent upon them my spent steam because— No, that was impossible.

"Hold on, my friend," I said, "stop where you are, let me pull myself together. This isn't their fault—" We were passing behind the screen hiding the little stage.

But he didn't hold on; he marched straight ahead; so did I, past the pitcher of ice water and the two last winter's palms, where he motioned me to a chair.

His introduction was not long, nor was it discursive. There was nothing eulogistic of my various acquirements, occupations, talents'; no remark about the optimistic trend of my literature, the affection in which my characters were held; nothing of this at all. Nor did I expect it. What interested me more was the man himself.

The steam of my wrath had blurred his outline and make-up before; now I got a closer, although a side, view of his person. He was a short man, much thicker at the middle than he was at either end—a defect all the more apparent by reason of a long-tailed, high-waisted, unbuttonable black coat which, while it covered his back and sides, would have left his front exposed, but for his snowy white waistcoat, which burst like a ball of cotton from its pod.

His only gesture was the putting together of his ten fingers, opening and touching them again to accentuate his sentences. What passed through my mind as I sat and watched him, was not the audience, nor what I was going to say to them, but the Christianlike self-control of this gentleman—a control which seemed to carry with it a studied reproof. Under its influence I unconsciously closed both furnace doors and opened my forced draft. Even then I should have reached for the safety-valve, but for an oily, martyr-like smile which flickered across his face, accompanied by a deprecating movement of his elbows, both indicating his patience under prolonged suffering, and his instant readiness to turn the other cheek if further smiting on my part was in store for him.

I strode to the edge of the platform:

"I know, good people," I exploded, "that you are not responsible for what has happened, but I want to tell you before I begin, that I have been boiling mad for ten minutes and am still at white heat, and that it is going to take me some time to get cool enough to be of the slightest service to you. You notice that I appear before you without a proper suit of clothes—a mark of respect which every lecturer should pay his audience. You are also aware that I am nearly an hour late. What I regret is, first, the cause of my frame of mind, second, that you should have been kept waiting. Now, let me tell you exactly what I have gone through, and I do it simply because this is not the first time that this has happened to your lecturers, and it ought to be your last. It certainly will be the last for me."

Then followed the whole incident, including

21

the Immaculate's protest about my being late, my explosion, etc., etc., even to the incident of my flask.

There was a dead silence—so dead and lifeless that I could not tell whether they were offended or not; but I made my bow as usual, and began my discourse.

The lecture over, the Immaculate paid me my fee with punctilious courtesy, waiving the customary receipt; followed me to the cloak-room, helped me on with my coat, picked up one of the bags, — an auditor the other, and the two followed me down Jacob's ladder into the night. Outside stood a sleigh shaped like the shell of Dr. Holmes's *Nautilus*, its body hardly large enough to hold a four-months-old baby. This was surrounded by half the audience, anxious, I afterward learned, for a closer view of the man who had "sassed" the Manager. Some of them expected it to continue.

I squeezed in beside the bags and was about to draw up the horse blanket, when a voice rang out :

"Mis' Plimsole's goin' in that sleigh, too." It was at Mrs. Plimsole's that I was to spend the night.

Then a faint voice answered back :

"No, I can just as well walk." She evidently

22

knew the danger of sitting next to an over-charged boiler.

Mrs. Plimsole!—a woman—walk—on a night like this—I was out of the sleigh before she had ceased to speak.

"No, madam, you are going to do nothing of the kind; if anybody is to walk it will be I; I'm getting used to it."

She allowed me to tuck her in. It was too dark for me to see what she was like—she was so swathed and tied up. Being still mad—fires drawn but still dangerous, I concluded that my companion was sour, and skinny, with a parrot nose and one tooth gone. That I was to pass the night at her house did not improve the esti-mate; there would be mottoes on the walls—"What is home without a mother," and the like; tidies on the chairs, and a red-hot stove smelling of drying socks. There would also be a basin and pitcher the size of a cup and saucer, and a bed that sagged in the middle and was covered with a cotton quilt.

The *Nautilus* stopped at a gate, beyond which was a smaller Jacob's ladder leading to a white cottage. Was there nothing built on a level in Sheffield? I asked myself. The bags which had been hung on the shafts came first, then I, then the muffled head and cloak. Upward and

onward again, through a door, past a pretty
girl who stood with her hand on the knob in
welcome, and into a hall. Here the girl helped
unmummy her mother, and then turned up the
hall-lamp.

Oh, such a dear, sweet gray-haired old lady!
The kind of an old lady you would have wanted
to stay—not a night with—but a year. An old
lady with plump fresh cheeks and soft brown
eyes and a smile that warmed you through and
through. And such an all-embracing restful
room with its open wood fire, andirons and polished fender—and the plants and books and
easy-chairs! And the cheer of it all!

"Now you just sit there and get comfortable,"
she said, patting my shoulder—(the second time
in one night that a woman's hand had been that
of an angel). "Maggie'll get you some supper.
We had it all ready, expecting you on the six-
ten. Hungry, aren't you?"

Hungry! I could have gnawed a hole in a sofa
to get at the straw stuffing.

She drew up a chair, waited till her daughter
had left the room, and said with a twinkle in
her eyes:

"Oh, I was glad you gave it to 'em the way
you did, and when you sailed into that snivelling
old Hard-shell deacon, I just put my hands down

24

under my petticoats and clapped them for joy.
There isn't anybody running anything up here.
They don't have to pay for this lecture course. It
was given to them by a man who is dead. All
they think they've got to do is to dress themselves up. They're all officers; there's a record-
ing secretary and a corresponding secretary and
an executive committee and a president and two
vice-presidents, and a lot more that I can't remember. Everyone of them is leaving everything
to somebody else to attend to. I know, because I
take care of all the lecturers that come. Only
last winter a lady lecturer arrived here on a load
of wood; she didn't lose her temper and get
mad like you did. Maybe you know her; she
told us all about the Indians and her husband,
the great general, who was surrounded and
massacred by them.''

"Know her, Madam, not only do I know and
love her, but the whole country loves her. She
is a saint, Madam, that the good Lord only allows
to live in this world because if she was trans-
ferred there would be no standard left.''

" Yes, but then you had considerable cause.
The hired girl next door—she sat next to my
daughter—said she didn't blame you a mite.''
(Somebody was on my side, anyhow.) ''Now
come in to supper.''

25

The next morning I was up at dawn: I had to get up at dawn because the omnibus made only one trip to the station, to catch the seven-o'clock train. I went by the eight-ten, but a little thing like that never makes any difference in Sheffield.

When the omnibus arrived it came on runners. Closer examination from the window of the cosey room — the bedroom was even more delightful — revealed a square furniture van covered on the outside with white canvas, the door being in the middle, like a box-car. I bade the dear old lady and her daughter good-by, opened the hall door and stood on the top step. The driver, a stout, fat-faced fellow, looked up with an inquiring glance.

"Nice morning," I cried in my customary cheerful tone — the dear woman had wrought the change.

"You bet! Got over your mad?"

The explosion had evidently been heard all over the village.

"Yes," I laughed, as I crawled in beside two other passengers.

"You was considerable het up last night, so Si was tellin' me," remarked the passenger, helping me with one bag.

I nodded. Who Si might be was not of special interest, and then again the subject had now lost its inflammatory feature.

The woman made no remark; she was evidently one of the secretaries.

"Well, by gum, if they had left me where they left you last night, and you a plumb stranger, I'd rared and pitched a little myself," continued the man. "When you come again—"

"Come again! Not by a—"

"Oh, yes, you will. You did them Hardshells a lot of good! You just bet your bottom dollar they'll look out for the next one of you fellows that comes up here!"

The woman continued silent. She would have something to say about any return visit of mine, and she intended to say it out loud if the time ever came!

The station now loomed into sight. I sprang out and tried the knob. I knew all about that knob—every twist and turn of it.

"Locked again!" I shouted, "and I've got to wait here an hour in this—"

"Hold on—*hold on*—" shouted back the driver. "Don't break loose again. I got the key."

My mail a week later brought me a county paper containing this statement: "The last lecturer, owing to some error on the part of the committee, was not met at the train and was considerably vexed. He said so to the audience and to the committee. Everybody was satisfied with his talk until they heard what they had to pay for it. He also said that he had left his dress suit in his trunk. If what we hear is true, he left his manners with it."

On reflection, the editor was right—*I had*.

A GENTLEMAN'S GENTLEMAN

I

I HAD left Sandy MacWhirter crooning over his smouldering wood fire the day Boggs blew in with news of the sale of Mac's two pictures at the Academy, and his reply to my inquiry regarding his future plans (vaguely connected with a certain girl in a steamer chair), "By the next steamer, my boy," still rang in my ears, but my surprise was none the less genuine when I looked up from my easel, two months later, at Sonning-on-the-Thames and caught sight of the dear fellow, with Lonnegan by his side, striding down the tow-path in search of me.

"By the Great Horn Spoon!" came the cry. And the next minute his big arms were about my shoulders, his cheery laugh filling the summer air.

Lonnegan's greeting was equally hearty and spontaneous, but it came with less noise.

"He's been roaring that way ever since we left London," said the architect. "Ever since we landed, really," and he nodded at Mac. "Awfully glad to see you, old man!"

29

The next moment the three of us were flat on the grass telling our experiences, the silver sheen of the river flashing between the low-branched trees lining the banks.

Lonnegan's story ran thus:

Mac had disappeared the morning after their arrival; had remained away two weeks, reappearing again with a grin on his face that had frozen stiff and had never relaxed its grip. "You can still see it; turn your head, Mac, and let the gentleman see your smile." Since that time he had spent his nights writing letters, and his days poring over the morning's mail. "Got his pocket full of them now, and is so happy he's no sort of use to anybody."

Mac now got his innings:

Lonnegan's airs had been insufferable and his ignorance colossal. What time he could spare from his English tailor — "and you just ought to see his clothes, and especially his checkerboard waistcoats" — had been spent in abusing everything in English art that wasn't three hundred years old, and going into raptures over Lincoln Cathedral. The more he saw of Lonnegan the more he was convinced that he had missed his calling. He might succeed as a floorwalker in a department store, where his airs and his tailor-made upholstery would impress the hayseeds from the country, but, as for trying to be— The rest was lost in a gurgle of smothered laughter, Lonnegan's thin, white fingers having by this time closed over the painter's windpipe.

My turn came now:

I had been at work a month; had my present quarters at the White Hart Inn, within a stone's throw of where we lay sprawled with our faces to the sun—the loveliest inn, by the way, on the Thames, and that was saying a lot—with hand-polished tables, sleeve and trouser-polished arm-chairs, Chippendale furniture, barmaids, pewter mugs, old and new ale, tough bread, tender mutton, tarts—gooseberry and otherwise; strawberries—two would fill a teacup—and *roses!* Millions of roses! "Well, you fellows just step up and look at 'em."

"And not a place to put your head," said Mac.

"How do you know?"

"Been there," replied Lonnegan. "The only decent rooms are reserved for a bloated American millionaire who arrives to-day—everything else chock-a-block except two bunks under the roof, full of spiders."

Mac drew up one of his fat legs, stretched his arms, pushed his slouch hat from his fore-

head—he was still on his back drinking in the
sunshine—and with a yawn cried:

"They ought to be exterminated."

"The spiders?" grumbled Lonnegan.

"No, millionaires. They throw their money
away like water; they crowd the hotels. Nothing good enough for them. Prices all doubled,
everything slimed up by the trail of their dirty
dollars. And the saddest thing in it all to me is
that you generally find one or two able-bodied
American citizens kotowing to them like wooden
Chinese mandarins when the great men take the
air."

"Who, for instance?" I asked. No millionaires with any such outfit had thus far come my
way.

"Lonnegan, for one," answered Mac.

The architect raised his head and shot a long,
horizontal glance at the prostrate form of the
painter.

"Yes, Lonnegan, I am sorry to say," continued Mac, his eyes fixed on the yellow greens in
the swaying tree-tops.

"I was only polite," protested the architect.
"Lambert is a client of mine; building a stable
for him. Very level-headed man is Mr. Samuel
Lambert; no frills and no swelled head. It was
Tommy Wing who was doing the mandarin act

32

the other day at the Carlton—not me. Got dead intimate with him on the voyage over and has stuck to him like a plaster ever since. Calls him 'Sam' already—did to me."

"Behind his back or to his face?" spluttered Mac, tugging at his pipe.

"Give it up," said Lonnegan, pulling his hat over his face to shield his eyes from the sun.

Mac raised himself to a sitting posture, as if to reply, fumbled in his watch-pocket for a match, instead; shook the ashes from his brier-wood, filled the bowl with some tobacco from his rubber pouch, drew the lucifer across his shoe, waited until the blue smoke mounted skyward and resumed his former position. He was too happy mentally—the girl in the steamer chair was responsible—and too lazy physically to argue with anybody. Lonnegan rolled over on his elbows, and feasted his eyes on the sweep of the sleepy river, dotted with punts and wherries, its background of foliage in silhouette against the morning sky. The Thames was very lovely that June, and the trained eye of the distinguished architect missed none of its beauty and charm. I picked up my brushes and continued work. The spirit of perfect camaraderie makes such silences not only possible but enjoyable. It is the restless chatterer that tires.

33

Lonnegan's outbreak had set me to thinking. Lambert I knew only by reputation—as half the world knew him—a man of the people: lumber boss, mill owner, proprietor of countless acres of virgin forest; many times a millionaire. Then came New York and the ice-cream palace with the rock-candy columns on the Avenue, and "The Samuel Lamberts" in the society journals. This was all the wife's doings. Poor Maria! She had forgotten the day when she washed his red flannel shirts and hung them on a line stretched from the door of their log cabin to a giant white pine—one of the founders of their fortune. If Tommy Wing called him "Sam" it was because old "Saw Logs," as he was often called, was lonely, and Tommy amused him.

Tommy Wing—Thomas Bowditch Wing, his card ran—I had known for years. He was basking on the topmost branches now, stretched out in the sunshine of social success, swaying to every movement made by his padrones. He was a little country squirrel when I first came across him, frisking about the root of the tree and glad enough to scamper close to the ground. He had climbed a long way since then. All the blossoms and tender little buds were at the top, and Tommy was fond of buds, especially when

34

they bloomed out into yachts and four-in-hands, country houses, winters in Egypt (Tommy an invited guest), house parties on Long Island or at Tuxedo, or gala nights at the opera with seats in a first tier.

In the ascent he had forgotten his beginnings —not an unnatural thing with Tommies: Son of a wine merchant—a most respectable man, too; then "Importer" (Tommy altered the sign); elected member of an athletic club; always well dressed, always polite;—invited to a member's house to dine; was unobtrusive and careful not to make a break. Asked again to fill a place at the table at the last moment— accepted gracefully, not offended—never offended at anything. Was willing to see that the young son caught the train, or would meet the daughter at the ferry and escort her safely to school. "So obliging, so trustworthy," the mother said. Soon got to be "among those present" at the Sherry and Delmonico balls. Then came little squibs in the society columns regarding the movements of Thomas Bowditch Wing, Esquire. He knew the squibber, and often gave her half a column. Was invited to a seat in the coaching parade, saw his photograph the next morning in the papers, he sitting next to the beautiful Miss Carnevelt. He was pretty near to

35

the top now; only a little farther to where the choicest buds were bursting into flower; too far up, though, ever to recognize the little fellows he had left frisking below. There was no time now to escort school-girls or fill unexpectedly empty seats unless they were exclusive ones. His excuse was that he had accepted an invitation to the branch above him. The mother of the school-girl now, strange to say, instead of being miffed, liked him the better, and, for the first time, began to wonder whether she hadn't made too free with so important a personage. As a silent apology she begged an invitation for a friend to the Bachelor Ball, Tommy being a subscriber and entitled to the distribution of a certain number of tickets. Being single and available, few outings were given without him — not only week-ends (Weak Odds-and-Ends, Mac always called them), but trips to Washington, even to Montreal in the winter. Then came the excursions abroad—Capri, Tangier, Cairo.

It was on one of these jaunts that he met "Saw Logs," who, after sizing him up for a day, promptly called him "Tommy," an abbreviation instantly adopted by Maria—so fine, you know, to call a fellow "Tommy" who knew everybody and went everywhere. Sometimes she shrieked his name the length of the deck. On reaching London it was either the Carlton or the Ritz for Lambert. Tommy, however, made a faint demur. "Oh, hang the expense, Tommy, you are my guest for the summer," broke out Lambert. What a prime minister you would have made, Tommy, in some kitchen cabinet!

There were no blossoms now out of his reach. Our little squirrel had gained the top! To dazzle the wife and daughter with the priceless value of his social position and then compel plain, honest, good-natured Samuel Lambert to pay his bills, and to pay those bills, too, in such a way, "by Heavens, sir, as not to wound a gentleman's pride": that, indeed, was an accomplishment. Had any other bushy tail of his acquaintance ever climbed so high or accomplished so much?

A movement on my right cut short my revery.

MacWhirter had lifted his big arms above his head, and was now twisting his broad back as if for a better fulcrum.

"Lonny—" he cried, bringing his body once more to a sitting posture.

"Yes, Mac."

"In that humiliating and servile interview which you had a short time ago with your other

37

genuflector, the landlord of the White Hart Inn, did you in any way gain the impression that every ounce of grub in his shebang was reserved for the special use of his highness, Count Kerosene, or the Earl of Asphalt, or the Duke of Sausage, or whatever the brute calls himself?—or do you think he can be induced to—"

"Yes, I think so."

"Think what, you obtuse duffer?"

"That he can be induced."

"Well, then, grab that easel and let us go to luncheon."

II

I had not exaggerated the charm of the White Hart Inn—nobody can. I know most of the hostelries up and down this part of the river—the "Ferry" at Cookham, the "French Horn" across the Backwater, one or two at Henley, and a lovely old bungalow of a tavern at Maidenhead; but this garden of roses at Sonning has never lost its fascination for me.

For the White Hart is like none of these. It fronts the river, of course, as they all do—you can almost fish out of the coffee-room window of the "Ferry" at Cookham—and all the life of the boat-houses, the punts and wherries, with their sprawling cushions and bunches of jack-straw oars, and tows, back and forth, of empty boats, goes on just as it does at the other boat-landings, up and down the river; but, at the White Hart, it is the rose garden that counts! Planted in rows, like corn, their stalks straight as walking-sticks and as big; then a flare of smaller stalks like umbrella ribs, the circle covered with Prince Alberts, Cloth-of-Golds, Teas, Saffrons, Red Ramblers (the old gardener knows their names; I don't). And the perfume that sweeps toward you and the way it sinks into your soul! Bury your face in a bunch of them, if you don't believe it.

Then the bridge! That mouldy old mass of red brick that makes three clumsy jumps before it clears the river, the green rushes growing about its feet. And the glory of the bend below, with the fluff of elm, birch and maple melting into the morning haze!

Inside it is none the less delightful. Awnings, fronting the garden, stretch over the flower-beds; vines twist their necks, the blossoms peeping curiously as you take your coffee.

There is a coffee-room, of course, with stags' heads and hunting prints, and small tables with old-fashioned flowers in tiny vases, as well as a long serving board the width of the room, where

everything that can be boiled, baked or stewed
and then served cold awaits the hungry.

It was at this long board that we three brought
up, and it was not long before Lonnegan and
Mac were filling their plates, and with their own
hands, too, with thin cuts of cold roast beef,
chicken and slivers of ham, picking out the particular bread or toast or muffin they liked best,
bringing the whole out under the low awning
with its screen of roses, the swinging blossoms
brushing their cheeks—some of them almost in
their plates.

From where we sat over our boiled and baked
—principally boiled—we could see not only the
suite of rooms reserved for the great man and
his party—one end of the inn, really, with a
separate entrance—but we could see, too, part
of the tap-room, with its rows of bottles, and could
hear the laughter and raillery of the barmaid as she
served the droppers-in and loungers-about. We
caught, as well, the small square hall, flanked by
the black-oak counter, behind which were banked
bottles of various shapes and sizes, rows of
pewter tankards and the like, the whole made
comfortable with chairs cushioned in Turkey
red, and never empty—the chairs, I mean;
the tankards always were, or about to be.

This tap-room, I must tell you, is not a bar in

the American sense, nor is the girl a barkeeper in any sense. It is the open club of the village, where everybody is welcome who is decent and agreeable. Even the curate drops in — not for his toddy, perhaps (although "You can't generally sometimes almost always tell," as Mac said), but for a word with anybody who happens to be about. And so does the big man of the village who owns the mill, and the gardener from Lord So-and-So's estate, and the lord himself, for that matter, the groom taking his "bitter" from the side window, with one eye on his high stepper polished to a piano finish. All have a word or a good-morning or a joke with the barmaid. She isn't at all the kind of a girl you think she is. Try it some day and you'll discover your mistake. It's Miss Nance, or Miss Ellen, or whatever else her parents fancied; or Miss Figgins, or Connors, or Pugby — but it is never Nance or Nell.

Our luncheon over, we joined the circle, the curate making room for Lonnegan, Mac stretching his big frame half over a settle.

"From the States, gentlemen, I should judge," said the curate in a cheery tone—an athletic and Oxford-looking curate, his high white collar and high black waistcoat gripping a throat and chest that showed oars and cricket bats in every muscle. Young, too—not over forty.

41

I returned the courtesy by pleading guilty, and in extenuation, presented my comrades to the entire room, Lonnegan's graceful body straightening to a present-arms posture as he grasped the outstretched hand of a brother athlete, and Mac's heartiness capturing every one present, including the barmaid.

Then some compounded extracts were passed over the counter and the talk drifted as usual (I have never known it otherwise) into comparisons between the two "Hands Across the Sea" people. That an Englishman will ever really warm to a Frenchman or a German nobody who knows his race will believe, but he can be entirely comfortable (and the well-bred Englishman is the shyest man living) with the well-bred American.

Lonnegan as chief spokesman, in answer to an inquiry, and with an assurance born of mastery of his subject instantly recognized by the listeners, enlarged on the last architectural horror, the skyscraper, its cost, and on the occupations of the myriads of human bees who were hived between its floors, all so different from the more modest office structures around the Bank of England: adding that he had the plans of two on his drawing table at home, a statement which confirmed the good opinions they had formed of his familiarity with the subject.

I floated in with some comparisons touching upon the technic of the two schools of water-color painting, and, finding that the curate had a brother who was an R.A., backed out again and rested on my oars.

Mac, more or less concerned over the expected arrival, and anxious that his listeners should not consider the magnate as a fair example of his countrymen, launched out upon the absence of all class distinctions at home— one man as good as another—making Presidents out of farmers, Senators out of cellar diggers, every man a king—that sort of thing.

When Mac had finished—and these Englishmen *let you finish*—the mill-owner, a heavy, red-faced man (out-of-doors exercise, not Burgundy), with a gray whisker dabbed high up on each cheek, and a pair of keen, merry eyes, threw back the lapels of his velveteen coat (riding-trousers to match), and answered slowly:

"You'll excuse me, sir, but I stopped a while in the States, and I can't agree with you. We take off our caps here to a lord because he is part of our national system, but we never bow down to the shillings he keeps in his strong box. You do."

The lists were "open" now. Mac fought valiantly, the curate helping him once in a

43

while; Lonnegan putting in a word for the several professions as being always exempt—brains, not money, counting in their case—Mac winning the first round with:

"Not all of us, my dear sir; not by a long shot. When any of our people turn sycophants, it is you English who have coached them. A lord with you is a man who doesn't have to work. So, when any of us come over here to play—and that's what we generally come for—everybody, to our surprise, kotows to us, and we acknowledge the attention by giving a shilling to whoever holds out his hand. Now, nobody ever kotows to us at home. We'd get suspicious right away if they did and shift our wallets to the other pocket; not that we are nct generous, but we don't like that sort of thing. We do here—that is, some of us do, because it marks the difference in rank, and we all, being kings, are tickled to death that your flunkies recognize that fact the moment they clap eyes on us."

Lonnegan looked at Mac curiously. The dear fellow must be talking through his hat.

"Now, I got a sudden shock on the steamer on my way home last fall, and from an *American gentleman*, too—one of the best, if he was in tarpaulins—and I didn't get over it for a week.

44

No kotow about him, I tell you. I wanted a newspaper the worst way, and was the first man to strike the Sandy Hook pilot as he threw his sea-drenched leg over the rail. 'Got a morning paper?' I asked. 'Yes, in my bag.' And he dumped the contents on the deck and handed me a paper. I had been away from home a year, mostly in England, and hadn't seen anybody, from a curator in a museum to the manager of an estate, who wouldn't take a shilling when it was offered him, and so from sheer force of habit I dropped a trade dollar into his hand. You ought to have seen his face. 'What's this for?' he asked. 'No use to me.' And he handed it back. I wanted to go out and kick myself full of holes, I was so ashamed. And, after all, it wasn't my fault. I learned that from you Englishmen."

The toot-toot of an automobile cut short the discussion.

The American millionaire had arrived!

Everybody now started on the run: landlord, two maids in blue dresses with white cap strings flying, three hostlers, two garage men, four dogs, all bowing and scraping—all except the dogs.

"What did I tell you?" laughed Mac, tapping the curate's broad chest with the end of his plump finger. "That's the way you all do. With us a porter would help him out, a hotel clerk assign him a room, and that would end it. The next morning the only man to do him reverence would be the waiter behind his chair figuring for the extra tip. Look at them. Same old kotow. No wonder he thinks himself a duke."

The party had disembarked now and were nearing the door of the private entrance, the two women in Mother Hubbard veils, the two men in steamer-caps and goggles—the valet and maid carrying the coats and parasols. The larger of the two men shed his goggles, changed his steamer-cap for a slouch hat which his valet handed him, and disappeared inside, followed by the landlord. The smaller man, his hands and arms laden with shawls and wraps, gesticulated for an instant as if giving orders to the two chauffeurs, waited until both machines had backed away, and entered the open door.

"Who do you think the big man is, Mac?" Lonnegan asked.

"Don't know, and don't want to know."

"Lambert."

"What! Saw Logs?"

"The same, and—yes—by Jove! That little fellow with the wraps is Tommy."

A moment later Tommy reappeared and made straight for the barmaid.

46

"Get me some crushed ice and vermouth," he said. "We carry our Hollands with us. Why, Mr. MacWhirter! and Mr. Lonnegan! and—" (I was the "and"—but he seemed to have forgotten my name.) "Well, this *is* a surprise!" Neither the mill-owner nor the curate came within range of his eyes.

"Where have I been? Well, I'll have to think. We did London for a week—Savoy for supper—Prince's for luncheon—theatre every night—that sort of thing. Picked up a couple of Gainsboroughs at Agnew's and some tapestries belonging to Lord —forget his name—had a letter." (Here Tommy fumbled in his pocket.) "No, I remember now, I gave it to Sam. Then we motored to Ravenstock—looked over the Duke's stables—spent the night with a very decent chap Sam met in the Rockies last year— son of Lord Wingfall, and—"

The ice was ready now (it was hived in a keg and hidden in the cellar, and took time to get at), and so was the vermouth and the glasses, all on a tray.

"No, I'll carry it." This to the barmaid, who wanted to call a waiter. "I never let anybody attend to this for Sam but myself"—this to us. "I'll be back in a minute."

In a few moments he returned, picking up the

thread of his discourse with: "Where was I? Oh, yes, at Lord Wingfall's son's. Well, that's about all. We are on our way now to spend a few days with—" Here he glanced at the curate and the mill-owner, who were absorbing every word that fell from his lips. "Some of the gentry in the next county—can't think of their names—friends of Sam." It became evident now that neither Mac nor Lonnegan intended introducing him to either of the Englishmen.

The barmaid pushed a second tray over the counter, and Tommy drew up a chair and waved us into three others. "Sam is so helpless, you know," he chatted on. "I can't leave him, really, for an hour. Depends on me for everything. Funny, isn't it, that a man worth— well, anywhere from forty to fifty millions of dollars, and made it all himself—should be that way? But it's a fact. Very simple man, too, in his tastes, when you know him. Mrs. Lambert and Rosie" (Mac stole a look at Lonnegan at the familiar use of the last name, but Tommy flowed on) "got tired of the *Cynthia*—she's a hundred and ninety feet over all, sixteen knots, and cost a quarter of a million—and wanted Sam to get something bigger. But the old man held out; wanted to know what I thought of it, and, of course, I had to say she was all right, and that settled it. Just the same way with that new house on the Avenue—you know it, Mr. Lonnegan—after he'd spent one hundred and fifty thousand dollars decorating the music-room— that's the one facing the Avenue —she thought she'd change it to Louis-Seize. Of course Sam didn't care for the money, but it was the dirt and plaster and discomfort of it all. By the way, after dinner, suppose you and Mr. Lonnegan, and you, too"—this to me—"come in and have a cigar with Sam. We've got some good Reina Victorias especially made for him—glad to have you know him."

Mac gazed out of the open door and shut his teeth tight. Lonnegan looked down into the custard-pie face of the speaker, but made no reply. Tommy laid a coin on the counter, shot out his cuffs, said : "See you later," and saun- tered out.

No! There were no buds or blossoms— noth- ing of any kind, for that matter —out of Tom- my's reach !

The mill-owner rose to his feet, straightened his square shoulders, made a movement as if to speak, altered his mind, shook Mac's hand warmly, and with a bow to the tap-room, and a special nod to the barmaid, mounted his horse

49

and rode off. The curate looked up and smiled, his gaze riveted on Mac.

"One of your American gentlemen, sir?" he asked. The tone was most respectful—not a trace of sarcasm, not a line visible about the corners of his mouth; only the gray eyes twinkled.

"No," answered Mac grimly; *"a gentleman's gentleman."*

The next morning at sunrise Mac burst into our room roaring with laughter, slapping his pajama-incased knee with his fat hand, the tears streaming from his eyes.

"They've gone!" he cried. "Scooted! Saw Logs, Mrs. Saw, the piece of kindling and her maid in the first car, and—"

He was doubled up like a jack-knife.

"And left Tommy behind!" we both cried.

"Behind!" Mac was verging on apoplexy now. "Behind! Not much. He was tucked away in the other car with the valet!"

ABIJAH'S BUBBLE

EZEKIEL TODD, her dry, tight-fisted, lean father, had named her, bawling it out so loud that the more suitable, certainly the more euphonious, "Evangeline," proffered in a timid whisper by her faded and somewhat romantic mother, was completely smothered.

"I baptize thee, Evang—" began the minister, when Ezekiel's voice rose clear:

"Abijah, I tell ye, Parson—A-b-i-j-a-h— Abijah!" And Abijah it was.

The women were furious.

"Jes' like Zeke Todd. He's too ornery to live. I come mighty near speakin' right out, and hadn't been that Martha held on to me I would. Call her Abbie, for short, Mrs. Todd," exclaimed Deacon Libby's wife, "and shame him."

Abbie never minded it. She was too little to remember, she always said, and there were few people in the village of Taylorsville present at the christening who did.

Old Si Spavey, however, never forgot. " You kin call yourself Abbie if you choose," he used to say, "and 'tain't none o' my business, but I was in the meetin'-house and heard Zeke let drive, and b'gosh it sounded just like a buzz-saw strikin' the butt-end of a log. ' Abijah! *Abijah!*' he hollered. Shet Parson Simmons up same's a steel trap. Gosh, but it was funny!"

Only twice since the christening had she to face the consequences of her father's ill temper. This was after his death, when the needs of the poor mother made a small mortgage imperative and she must sign as a witness. It came with a certain shock, but there was no help for it, and she went through the ordeal bravely, dotting the "i" and giving a little flourish to the tail of the "h."

The second time was when she signed her application for the position of postmistress of the village. The big mill-owner, Hiram Taylor, brought her the paper.

"Got to put it all in, Miss Abbie," he said with a laugh. "Shut your eyes and sign it and then forget it. Awful, ain't it? — but that's the law, and there ain't no way of getting round it, I guess."

Hiram Taylor had left the village years before, rather suddenly, some had thought, when he was a strapping young fellow of twenty-two or

52

three, and had moved West and stayed West until he came back the year before with a wife and a houseful of children. Then the lawyers in the village got busy, and pretty soon some builders came down from Boston, only fifty miles away, and then a lot of brick-layers; and some cars were switched off on the siding, loaded with lumber and lath and brick, and next a train-load of machinery, and so the mills were running again with Hiram sole owner and in full charge. One of the first things he did after his arrival — the following morning, really — was to look up Abbie's mother. He gave a little start when he saw how shabby the cottage looked; no paint for years — steps rot-ting — window-blinds broken, with a hinge loose. He gave a big one when a thin, hollow-chested woman, gray and spare, opened the door at his knock.

"Hiram!" she gasped, and the two went in-side, and the door was shut.

All she said when Abbie came home from school — she was teaching that year — was: "The new mill-owner came to see me. His name's Taylor."

That same day a heavy-set man with gray hair and beard, and jet-black eyebrows shading two kindly eyes, got out of his wagon, hitched

53

his horse to a post in front of the school-house and stepped to Abbie's desk.

"I'm Hiram Taylor, up to the mills. Going to send one of my girls to you to-morrow and thought I'd drop in." Then he looked around and said: "Want another coat of whitewash on these walls, don't you, and—and a new stove? This don't seem to be drawin' like it ought to. If them trustees won't get ugly about it, I got a new stove up to the mill I don't want, and I'll send it down." And he did. The trustees shrugged their shoulders, but made no objections. If Hiram Taylor wanted to throw his money away it was none of their business. Abbie Todd never said she was cold—not as they had "heard on."

When the new school building was finished —a brick structure with stone trimmings, steam-heated, and varnished desks and seats—the craze for the new and up-to-date so dominated the board that they paid Abbie a month's salary in advance and then replaced her with a man graduate from Concord. Abbie took her dismissal as a matter of course. Nothing good ever lasted long. When she went up one step she always slid back two. It had been that way all her life.

Hiram heard of it and came rattling into the

54

village, where he expressed himself at a town meeting in language distinguished for its clearness and force. The result was Abbie's application for the position of postmistress.

This time he didn't consult the trustees or anybody else. He wrote a private note to the Postmaster-General, who was his friend, and the appointment came by return mail.

Mr. Taylor would often chat with her through the little window with which she held converse with the public — he often came himself for his mail — but she made no mention of her state of mind. She was earning her living, and she was for the time content. He had helped her and she was grateful — more than this it was not her habit to dwell upon. One thing she was convinced of: she wouldn't keep the position long.

Her mother knew her misgivings, and so did a small open wood fire in the sitting-room. Many a night the two would croon together. The mother shrivelled and faded; Abbie herself being over thirty — not so fresh-looking as she had been — not so pretty — never had been very pretty. Her mother knew, too, how hard she had always struggled to do something better; how she had studied drawing at the normal school when she was preparing to be a teacher; and how she had spent weeks in the elaboration

55

of wall-paper patterns, which she had sent to the
Decorative Art Society in Boston, only to have
them returned to her in the same wrapper in
which they had been mailed, with the indorse-
ment "not suitable." That's why she didn't
think she was going to be postmistress long.
Far into the night these talks would continue—
long after the other neighbors had gone to bed
—nine o'clock maybe—sometimes as late as ten
—an unheard-of thing in Taylorsville, where
everybody was up at daylight.

Then one day an extraordinary thing happened—extraordinary so far as her modest post-
office was concerned. A poster appeared on the
wall of her office—a huge card, big as the top
of a school desk, bearing in large type this le-
gend: "Rock Creek Copper Company. Keep
& Co., Agents," and at the bottom, in small
type, directions as to the best way of securing
the stock before the lists were closed. She had
noticed the name of the company emblazoned
on many of the communications addressed to
people in the village—the richer ones—but here
it was in cold type—"hot type," for that
matter, for it was in flaming red—on the wall,
in front of her window.

Abbie lifted her head in surprise when she saw
what had been done without even "By your

leave." She had found auction sales, sheriff's notices and tax warnings opposite her window, but never copper mines. The longer she looked at it the better she liked it. There was a cheery bit of color in its blazing letters, and she was partial to bits of color. That's why she kept plants all winter in the little sitting-room at home, and nursed one cactus that gave out a scarlet bloom once in so many months.

It was Miss Maria Furgusson, of Boston—summer boarder at the next cottage; second floor, six dollars a week, including washing—that revived, kept alive, in fact, fanned to fever heat, Abbie's first impression of the poster. Maria called for her mail, and the intimacy had gone so far that before the week was out "Miss Todd" had been replaced by "Abbie" and then "Ab," and Miss Furgusson by "Maria"—the postmistress being too dignified for further abbreviation.

"Oh, there's our lovely copper mine—where did you get it? Who put it up?"

Maria was a shirt-waisted young woman with a bang and a penetrating voice. She had charge of the hosiery counter in a department store and could call "Cash" in tones that brought instant service. This, with her promptness, had endeared her to many impatient customers—especially those from out of town who wanted to

57

catch trains. It was through one of these "hayseeds" that she secured board at so reasonable a price in Taylorsville during her vacation.

"What do you know about it?" inquired Abbie. Such things were Greek to her.

"Know? I've got twenty shares, and I'm going to have money to burn before long."

Abbie bent her head, and took in as much of Miss Furgusson as she could see through the square hole in her window.

"Who gave it to you?" The idea of a girl like Maria ever having money enough to buy anything of that kind never occurred to her.

"Nobody; I bought it; paid two dollars a share for it and now it's up to three, and Mr. Slathers, our floor-walker, says it's going to twenty-five. I've got a profit of twenty dollars on mine now."

Abbie made a mental calculation; twenty dollars was a considerable part of her month's salary.

"And everybody in our store has got some. Mr. Slathers has made eight hundred dollars, and I know for sure that Miss Henders is going to leave the cloak department and set up a type-writing place, because she told me so; she's got a brother in the feed business who staked her."

58

"Staked her? What's that?"

"Loaned her the money," answered Maria, a certain pity in her voice for one so green and countrified.

"How do you get it?" Abbie's eyes were shining like the disks of a brass letter scale and almost as large—they were still upon Maria.

"The money?"

"No, the stock."

"Why, send Mr. Keep the money and he buys the stock and sends you back the certificate. Want to see mine? I've got it pinned in— Here it is."

Abbie opened the door of the glass partition and beckoned to the shopgirl. She rarely allowed visitors inside, but this one seemed to hold the key to a new world.

The girl slipped her fingers inside her shirt-waist and drew out a square piece of paper bearing the inscription of the poster in big letters. At the bottom of the paper a section of cement drain-pipe poured forth a steady stream of water, and the whole was underlined by a motto meaning "Peace and Plenty"—of water, no doubt.

Abbie looked at the beautifully engraved document and a warm glow suffused her face. Was it as easy as this? Did this little scrap of paper

59

mean rest and the spreading of wings, and freedom for her mother? Then she caught her
breath. She hadn't any brother in the feed
business—nor anywhere else, for that matter.
How would she get the money? She had only
her salary; her mother earned little or nothing—
the interest on the mortgage would be due in a
day or so; thank God it was nearly paid off.
Then her heart rose in her throat. Mr. Taylor!
Why he was so kind she never knew—but he
was. But if he insisted as he had with the
store and the position in the post-office! No
—he had done too much already. Besides, she
could never repay him if anything went wrong.
No—this was not her chance for freedom.

Abbie handed the certificate back. "Queer
way of making money," was all she said as she
reached for her hat and shawl, and went home
to dinner.

That evening after supper, the two crooning
over the fire, Abbie talked it over with her
mother—not the stock—not a word of that—
but of how Maria had made a lot of money, and
how she wished she had a little of her own so
she could make some, too. This the mother
retailed, the next morning, to her neighbor, who
met the expressman, who thereupon sent it roll-
ing through the village. In both its diluted and

60

enriched form the neighbor had helped. The story was as follows:

"That Boston girl who was boardin' up to Skitson's had a thousand dollars in the bank— made it all in a month— so Abbie Todd, who knew her, said. It was a dead secret how she made it, but Abbie said if she had a few hundred dollars she could get rich, too. Beats all how smart some girls is gettin' to be nowadays."

The next morning Mr. Taylor called for his mail. He generally sent a boy down from the mill, but this time he came himself.

"If you see anything lying around loose, Miss Abbie, where you can pick up a few dollars —and you must now and then—so many people going in and out from Boston and other places—and want a couple of hundred to help out, let me know. I'll stake you, and glad to."

In answer, Abbie passed his mail through the square window. "Thank you, Mr. Taylor," was all she said. "I won't forget."

Hiram fingered his mail and hung around for a minute. Then with the remark: "Guess that expressman was lying—I'll find out, anyway," he got into his buggy and drove away.

"He'll *stake* me, will he?" said Abbie thoughtfully. "That's what the feed man did for Maria's friend." With the stake she could get the stock, and with the stock the clouds would lift! Perhaps her turn was coming, after all.

Then she resumed her work pigeon-holing the morning's mail. One was from Keep & Co., judging from the address in the corner, and was directed to Maria Furgusson, care Miss Skitson — a thick, heavy letter. This she laid aside.

"Yes, a big one," she called from the window as she passed it out to that young woman five minutes later. "About the stock, isn't it!"

The girl tore open the envelope and gave a little scream.

"Oh! Gone up to ten dollars a share! Oh, cracky!—how much does that make? Here, Ab—do you figure—twenty shares at—Ten! Why, that's two hundred dollars! What?—it can't be! Yes, it is. Oh, that's splendid! I'm going right back to answer his letter"—and she was gone.

When the supper things were washed up that night, and the towels hung before the stove to dry, and the faded old mother was resting in her chair by the fire, Abbie told her the facts as they existed. She had seen the certificate with her own eyes—had had it in her hand and she had read the letter from the broker, Mr. Keep. It was all true—every word of it. Maria had borrowed forty dollars and now she could pay it back and have one hundred and sixty dollars left — more than she herself could earn in three months.

"If I could get somebody to lend me a little money, Mother," she continued, "I might—"

The girl stopped and stole a look at her mother sitting hunched up in her chair, her elbows on her knees, the chin resting on the palms of her hands, the angle of her thin shoulders outlined through the coarse, worsted shawl—always a pathetic attitude to the daughter:—this old mother broken with hard work and dulled by a life of continued disappointment.

"I was saying, Mother, perhaps I might get somebody to lend me a little money, and then—"

The figure straightened up. "Don't do it, child!" There was a note almost of terror in her voice. "Don't you ever do it! That was what ruined my father. Abbie—promise me—promise me, I say! You won't—you can't."

The girl laid her hand tenderly on her mother's shoulder.

" Why, Mother, dear—why, what's the matter? You look as if you had seen a ghost."

Mrs. Todd drew her shawl closer about her shoulders and leaned nearer to the girl, her voice trembling:

63

"It's worse than a ghost, child—it's a *debt!*
Debt along of money you never worked for;
money somebody gives you sort o' friendly-like,
and when you can't pay it back, they bite you,
like dogs. No—let's sit here and starve first,
child. We can shut the door and nobody 'll
know we're hungry." She straightened up and
threw the shawl from her shoulders. Terror
had taken the place of an undefined dread.

"You ain't gettin' discouraged, Abbie, be
you?" she continued in a calmer tone. "Don't
get discouraged, child. I got discouraged when
I was younger than you, and I ain't never been
happy since. You never knew why, and I ain't
goin' to tell you now, but it's been black night
all these years—all 'cept you. You've been the
only thing made me live. If you get discouraged,
child, I can't stand it. Say you ain't, Abbie—
let me hear you say it—please Abbie!"

The girl rose from her chair and stood looking
down at her mother. The sudden outburst,
so unusual in one so self-restrained, the unmis-
takable suffering in the tones of her voice,
thrilled and alarmed her. Her first impulse was
to throw her arms about her mother's neck and
weep with her. This had been her usual custom when the load seemed too heavy for her
mother to bear. Then the more practical side

64

of her nature asserted itself. It was strength, not sympathy, she wanted. Slipping her hand under her mother's arm, she raised her to her feet, and in a firm, decided voice, quite as a hospital nurse would speak to a restless patient, she said:

"You'd better not sit up any longer, Mother dear. Come, I'll help put you to bed."

There was no resistance. Whatever suddenly aroused memory had stirred the outburst, the paroxysm was over now.

"Well, maybe I am tired, child," was all she said, and the two left the room.

"Poor, dear old Mother! Poor, tired old Mother!" the girl remarked to herself when she had resumed her place by the dying fire. "Wonder if I'll get that way when I'm as old as she is!"

Then the hopelessness of the struggle she was making rose before her. How much longer would this go on? Up at six o'clock; a cup of coffee and a piece of bread; then the monotonous sorting of letters and papers—the ceaseless answering of stupid questions; then half an hour for dinner; then the routine again till train time, and home to the mother and the two chairs by the fire, only to begin the dreary tread-mill again the next morning. And with this the daily growing older — older; her face thinner and more pinched, the shoulders sharp; her hair gray, head bent, just as her poor mother's was, and, with all that, hardly money enough to buy herself a pair of shoes — never enough to give her dear mother the slightest luxury.

Discouraged! Hadn't she reason to be?

The next morning Hiram walked into the post-office and called to Abbie, through the square window, to open the door. Once inside he loosened his fur driving-coat, took out a long, black wallet, picked out a thin slip of paper and laid it on Abbie's desk.

"I have been thinking over what I told you yesterday. There's a check drawn to your order for two hundred dollars. All you got to do is to put your name on the back of it and it's money. It's good — never knew one that warn't."

The girl started back.

"I didn't ask you for it. I don't—"

"I know you didn't, and when you did it would be too late maybe — got to catch things sometimes when they're flying past. I don't know whether it's those town lots they're booming over to Haddam's Corners, and I don't care, but if that ain't enough there's more where that came from. Good-day!" and he slammed the glass door behind him.

Abbie picked up the thin slip of paper and studied every line on its face, from the red number in the upper corner to "Hiram Taylor" in a bold, round hand. Then her eyes lighted on "Abijah Todd or order."

Yes, it was hers—all of it. Not to spend, but to *make money out of*. Then her mother's words of warning rang clear: "Worse than a ghost, my child!" Should she—could she take it? She turned to lay it in a drawer until she could hand it back to him and her eyes fell upon the poster framed in by the square of her window. She stopped and shut the drawer. Was she never to have her chance? Would the treadmill never end? Would the dear mother's head never be lifted? Folding the check carefully, she loosened the top button of her dress and pushed it inside. There it burned like a hot coal.

That night, after putting her mother to bed, she pinned a shawl over her head, threw her mother's cloak about her shoulders, sneaked into Maria's house, and crept up into her friend's room like a burglar. What was to be done must be done quickly, but intelligently.

"I've got some money," she exclaimed to the astonished girl who, half undressed, sat writing at her table. (It was after nine o'clock—an unheard-of hour for visiting.) "How much stock can I buy for two hundred dollars?" and she shook out the check, keeping her finger over the signature.

"Twenty shares," answered Maria.

"How do I get it?"

"Send the money to Keep & Co. Oh, you got a check! Well, put 'Keep & Co.' on— here, I'll do it, and you sign your name underneath. And I'll write 'em a letter and tell 'em I helped sell it to you. Oh, ain't I glad, Ab. You must be getting awful big pay to have saved all that. Wish I—"

"How long before I know?" She had not much time to talk—her mother might wake and call her.

"They'll telephone you. You got a long-distance, ain't you, in the office? Yes, I seen it."

Abbie took the name of the senior partner, replaced the check, and was by her own fire again. The mother hadn't stirred.

All the next day she waited for the rattle of the bell. At three o'clock she sprang to the 'phone.

"This Miss Todd—postmistress?"

"Yes."

68

"Got your check—bought you twenty Rock Creek at ten—mail you certificate to-morrow."

The following morning the certificate took the place of the check—pinned tight. She could feel it crinkle when she walked. All that day she moved about her office like one dazed. There was no exaltation—no thrill of triumph. A dull, undefined terror took possession of her. What if the stock went down in price and she couldn't pay back the money? Of whom, then, could she borrow? Repay Hiram she must and would. Again her mother's warning words rang in her ears. Then came the resolve never to tell her. If it went right she would add to the dear woman's comforts in silence. If it went wrong—but it couldn't go wrong: Maria had said so: the papers had said so: the posters said so—everybody and everything said so.

As the day wore on she became so nervous that she mixed the letters in their pigeon-holes.

"That ain't for me, Miss Todd," was called out half a dozen times when B or F or S letters had gone into the wrong box. "Guess you must a-got it in the B's by mistake. Wool-gatherin', ain't ye?"

Maria was her only confidante and her only comfort. The Boston girl laughed when she listened to her fears, and braced her up with

fairy stories of the winnings of Miss Henders
and Slathers and the money they were making;
but the relief was only temporary.

Soon the strain began to show itself in her
face. "You ain't sick, Abbie, be you?" asked
the mother. "No? Well, you look kind o'
peaked. Don't work too hard, child. Maybe
something's worryin' you—something you ain't
told me. No man I don't know about, is there?"
and the mother's sad eyes searched the daughter's.

To all these inquiries the girl only shook her
head, adding that the down mail was late and a
big one and she had hurried to sort it.

When the Boston mail arrived the next morning and was dumped from its bag upon her sort-
ing-table, her own name flamed out on one of
Keep & Co.'s envelopes.

Abbie broke the seal and devoured its contents with bated breath, her fingers trembling:

We are happy to inform you that the last
sales of Rock Creek ranged from 13 to 14¾ —
15 bid at close. We confidently expect the
stock will sell at 20 before the week is out. We
shall be glad to receive your further orders as
well as those of any of your friends.

Abbie's heart gave a bound; the blood
mounted to the roots of her hair.

" Fifteen — twenty — why — why! that's two hundred dollars for me after paying Mr. Taylor." The chill of doubt was over now. The fever of hope had set in. "Two hundred! Two hundred!" she kept repeating, as her fingers caressed the certificate snuggling close to her heart.

When she swung wide the porch door and threw her arms around her astonished mother's neck, the refrain was still on her lips. It had been years since the hard-working girl had given way to any such joyous outburst.

"Oh, I'm so happy! Don't ask me why — but I am!"

The mother kissed her in reply and patted the girl's shoulder. "There *is* somebody," she sighed to herself. "And they've made up again"—and a prayer trembled on her lips.

Her joy now became contagious. The expressman noticed it; so did Mrs. Skitson and the storekeeper. So did Mr. Taylor, who stopped his wagon and leaned half out to shake her hand.

"You do look wholesome this morning, and no mistake, Miss Abbie" (he always called her so). "Don't forget what I told you—lots more where that come from "—and he drove on muttering to himself: "Ain't no finer woman in Taylorsville than Abbie Todd."

71

Keep & Co. letters arrived now by almost every mail. With these came a daily stock-list printed on tissue-paper, giving the sales on the exchange. Rock Creek was still holding its own between 13 and 15. "From my brokers," she would say with a smile to Maria, falling into the ways of the rich.

One of these letters, marked "Private and confidential," she took to Maria. It was in the writer's own hand and signed by the senior member of the firm. Literally translated into uncommercial language by that female financier, it meant that Miss Todd, "*on notice from Keep & Co.*" should write her name at the bottom of the transfer blank on the back of the certificate and mail it to them. This done they would buy her another ten shares of stock, using her certificate as additional margin. There was no question that Rock Creek would sell at forty before the month ended, and they did not want her to be "left" when the "melon was cut."

Another and a newer and a more vibrant song now rose to her lips. Forty for Rock Creek meant four — six — yes, eight hundred dollars — with two hundred to Mr. Taylor! Yes! Six hundred clear! The scrap of paper in her bosom was no longer a receipt for money paid, but an Aladdin's lamp producing untold wealth.

That night the music burst from her lips before she had taken off her cloak and hat.

"You made six hundred dollars, Abbie! *You!*" cried the mother, with a note of wonder in her voice.

Then the whole story came out; her mother's arms about her, the pale cheek touching her own, tears of joy streaming from both their eyes. First Maria's luck, then that of her fellow-clerks; then the letters, one after another, spread out upon her lap, the lamp held close, so the dim eyes could read the easier—down to the stake-money of two hundred dollars.

"And who gave you that, child? Miss Furgusson?" The mother's heart was still fluttering. After all, the sun was shining.

"No; Mr. Taylor."

The mother put her hands to her head.

"*Hiram!* You ain't never borrowed any money of Hiram, have you?" she cried in an agonized voice.

"But, Mother dear, he forced it upon me. He came—"

"Yes. that's what he did to me. Give it back to him, child, now, 'fore you sleep. Don't wait a minute. Borrowed two hundred dollars of Hiram—and my child, too! Oh, it can't be! It can't be!

73

The mother dropped into a chair and rocked herself to and fro. The girl started to explain, to protest, to comfort her with promises; then she crossed to where her mother was sitting, and stood patient until the paroxysm should pass. A sudden fright now possessed her; these attacks were coming on oftener; was her mother's mind failing? Was there anything serious? Perhaps it would have been better not to tell her at all.

The mother motioned Abbie to a chair.

"Sit down, child, and listen to me. I ain't crazy; I ain't out of my head—I'm only skeered."

"But, Mother dear, I can get the money any day I want it. All I've got to do is to telephone them and a check comes the next day."

"Yes, I know—I know." She was still trembling, her voice hardly audible. "But that ain't what skeers me; it's Hiram. He done the same thing to me last December. Come in here and laid the bills on that table behind you and begged me to take 'em; he'd heard about the mortgage; he wanted to fix the house up, too. I put my hands behind my back and got close to the wall there. I couldn't touch it, and he begged and begged, and then he went away. Next he went to the school-house, and you know what he did. That's why you got the post-office."

A light broke in upon the girl. "And you've known him before?"

"Yes, forty years ago. He loved me and I loved him. We had bad luck, and my father got into trouble. He and Hiram's father were friend's; been boys together, and Hiram's father loaned him money. I don't know how much — I never knew, but considerable money. My father couldn't pay, and then come bad blood. The week before Hiram and I were to be called in church they struck each other, and when Hiram took my father's part his father drove him out of his house, and Hiram hadn't nothing, and went West; and I never heard from him nor saw him till the day he come in here last fall. Don't you see, child, you got to take him back his money?"

Abbie squared her shoulders. The blood of the Puritan was in her eyes. This was a fight for home and freedom. Her flintlock was between the cracks of her log cabin. The old mother, with the other women and children, lay huddled together in the far corners. This was no time for surrender!

"No!" she cried in a firm voice. "I won't give it back, not till I get good and ready. Mr.

Taylor loaned me that two hundred dollars to make money with, and he won't get it again till I do." She wondered at her courage, but it seemed the only way to save her mother from herself. "What happened forty years ago has nothing to do with what's happening to-day."

The look in the girl's eyes; her courage; the ring of independence in her voice, the sureness and confidence of her words, began to have their effect. The Genie of the Lamp was at work: the life-giving power of Gold was being pumped from her own into the poor old woman's poverty-shrunken veins.

"And you don't think, child, that it will bring you trouble?"

"Bring trouble!" No!

The cabin was saved; the enemy was in retreat. She could sing once more! "It will bring nothing but joy and freedom, you precious old Mother! Do you know what I'm going to do?"

"What, child?"

"I'm going to pay off the mortgage, every cent of it."

(She said "I" now; it had been "we" all the years before : Keep rubbing, dear old Genie). "Then I'll fix up the house and paint it, and

76

get you some nice clothes, and a new cook stove that isn't all rusted out——"

"You won't resign, will you, Abbie—and leave me?" the mother exclaimed. The chill of possible desertion suddenly crept over her, (The Genie is often unmindful of others, especially the poor.)

"Leave you! What, now? You darling Mother. As to resigning, I may later. But I'm going to Boston when I get my vacation and stay a week with Maria, and go to the opera if I never do another thing. Oh! just you wait, Mother, you and I will lead a different life after this."

"And you think, Abbie, you'll make more than six hundred dollars?" Already the mother's veins were expanding—wonderful elixir, this Extract of Gold.

"Six hundred! Why, if the stock goes to what they call par—and that's where they all go, so Maria says—I'll have—have—two thousand, less Mr. Taylor's two hundred—I'll have eighteen hundred dollars!" The little fellow in her bosom was rubbing away now with all his might. She could hear his heart beat against her own.

It was nearly midnight when the two went to bed. Stick after stick had been thrown on the fire; the logs had flamed and crackled in sympathy with their own joyous feelings, and had then fallen into piled-up coals, each heap a castle of delight, rosy in the glow of freshly enkindled hopes.

And the song in her heart never ceased. Day by day a fresh note was added; everything she touched; everything she saw was transformed. The old tumble-down house with its propped-up furniture and makeshift carpets seemed to have become already the place she planned it to be. There would be vines over the door and a new summer kitchen at the back; and there would be a porch where her mother could sit, flowers all about her—her dear mother, bent no longer, but fresh and rosy in her new clothes, smiling at her as she came up the garden path.

And what delight it was just to breathe the air! Never had her step been so light, or her daily walk to the dingy office — dingy no longer — so bracing. And the out-of-doors — the sky and drifting clouds; the low hills, bleak in the winter's gloom — what changes had come over them? Was it the first blush of the coming spring that had softened their lines, or had her eyes been blind to all their beauty? Oh! Marvellous elixir that makes hope a certainty and gilds each cloud!

One morning a man waiting for a letter from an absent son heard the telephone ring, and saw Abbie drop her letters and catch up the receiver:

"Yes, I'm Miss Todd.— Oh! Mr. Keep? Yes.— Yes— I've got it here." Her face grew deathly white. "What! Selling at twelve!" The man feared she was about to fall. "I thought you told me . . . A big slump! Well, I don't want to lose if . . . Yes, I'll mail it right away . . . Reach you by the 9. 10 to-morrow."

"I hope you ain't got any bad news, have you?" the man asked in a sympathetic voice.

"No," she answered in a choking voice, as she handed him his letter; then she turned her back and took the certificate from her bosom.

"Selling at twelve," she kept saying to herself; "perhaps at ten; perhaps at five. Would it go lower? Suppose it went down to nothing. What could she say to her mother? How would she pay Mr. Taylor? Her breath came short; a dull sense of some impending calamity took possession of her. Everything seemed slipping from her grasp.

An hour passed — two. In the interim she had indorsed the certificate and had dropped it into the open mouth of the night-bag. Again the bell sounded.

"Yes," she answered in a faint voice; her shoulder was against the wall now for support.

79

She was ready for the blow; all her life they had come this way.

"Sold your twenty at ten. Mail you check for $190 on receipt of certificate."

Abbie clutched her bosom as if for relief, but there came no answering throb. The little devil was gone, and the lamp with him.

.   .   .   .

"And is it all over, Abbie?" asked her mother, as she drew her shawl closer about her head. One stick of wood must last them till bedtime now.

"Yes — all." The girl lay crouched at her feet sobbing, her head in her mother's lap.

"Can you pay Hiram?"

"I have paid him in full. I gave him Mr. Keep's check and ten dollars of my pay — paid him this morning. He wouldn't take any interest."

"Oh, that's good — that's good, child!" she crooned.

There came a long pause, during which the two women sat motionless, the mother looking into the smouldering coals. She had but few tears left   none for disappointments like these.

"And we have got to keep on as we have?"

"Yes." The reply was barely audible.

The mother lifted her thin, worn hand, and laid it on Abbie's head.

"Well, child," she said slowly, "you can thank God for one thing. *You had your dream;* ain't many even had that."

A LIST TO STARBOARD

I

A SHORT, square chunk of a man walked into a shipping office on the East Side, and inquired for the Manager of the Line. He had kindly blue eyes, a stub nose, and a mouth that shut to like a rat-trap, and stayed shut. Under his chin hung a pair of half-moon whiskers which framed his weather-beaten face as a spike collar frames a dog's.

"You don't want to send this vessel to sea again," blurted out the chunk. "She ought to go to the dry-dock. Her boats haven't had a brushful of paint for a year; her boilers are caked clear to her top flues, and her pumps won't take care of her bilge water. Charter something else and lay her up."

The Manager turned in his revolving chair and faced him. He was the opposite of the Captain in weight, length, and thickness—a slim, well-groomed, puffy-cheeked man of sixty with a pair of uncertain, badly aimed eyes and a voice like the purr of a cat.

"Oh, my dear Captain, you surely don't

mean what you say. She is perfectly sea-
worthy and sound. Just look at her inspection —" and he passed him the certificate.

"No — I don't want to see it! I know 'em by
heart: it's a lie, whatever it says. Give an in-
spector twenty dollars and he's stone blind."

The Manager laughed softly. He had handled
too many rebellious captains in his time; they
all had a protest of some kind — it was either the
crew, or the grub, or the coal, or the way she
was stowed. Then he added softly, more as a
joke than anything else:

"Not afraid, are you, Captain ?"

A crack started from the left-hand corner of
the Captain's mouth, crossed a fissure in his
face, stopped within half an inch of his stub
nose, and died out in a smile of derision.

"What I'm afraid of is neither here nor there.
There's cattle aboard — that is, there will be by
to-morrow night; and there's a lot of passengers
booked, some of 'em women and children. It
isn't honest to ship 'em and you know it! As to
her boilers send for the Chief Engineer. He'll
tell you. You call it taking risks; I call it mur-
der!"

"And so I understand you refuse to obey the
orders of the Board? — and yet she's got to sail
on the 16th if she sinks outside."

83

"When I refuse to obey the orders of the Board I'll tell the Board, not you. And when I do tell 'em I'll tell 'em something else, and that is, that this chartering of worn-out tramps, painting 'em up and putting 'em into the Line, has got to stop, or there'll be trouble."

"But this will be her last trip, Captain. Then we'll overhaul her."

"I've heard that lie for a year. She'll run as long as they can insure her and her cargo. As for the women and children, I suppose they don't count—" and he turned on his heel and left the office.

On the way out he met the Chief Engineer.

"Do the best you can, Mike," he said; "orders are we sail on the 16th."

On the fourth day out this conversation took place in the smoking-room between a group of passengers.

"Regular tub, this ship!" growled the Man-Who-Knew-It-All to the Bum Actor. "Screw out of the water every souse she makes; lot of dirty sailors skating over the decks instead of keeping below where they belong; Chief Engineer loafing in the Captain's room every chance he gets —there he goes now—and it's the second time since breakfast. And the Captain is no better!

84

And just look at the accommodations — three stewards and a woman! What's that to look after thirty-five passengers? Half the time I have to wait an hour to get something to eat — such as it is. And my bunk wasn't made up yesterday until plumb night. That bunch in the steerage must be having a hard time."

"We get all we pay for," essayed the Travelling Man. "She ain't rigged for cabin passengers, and the Captain don't want 'em. Didn't want to take me — except our folks had a lot of stuff aboard. Had enough passengers, he said."

"Well, he took the widow and her two kids —" continued the Man-Who-Knew-It-All — "and they were the last to get aboard. Half the time he's playing nurse instead of looking after his ship. Had 'em all on the bridge yesterday."

"He *had* to take 'em," protested the Travelling Man. "She was put under his charge by his owners — so one of the stewards told me."

"Oh! — *had to*, did he! Yes — I've been there before. No use talking — this line's got to be investigated, and I'm going to do the investigating as soon as I get ashore, and don't you forget it! What's your opinion?"

The Bum Actor made no reply. He had been cold and hungry too many days and nights to find fault with anything. But for the generosity of a few friends he would still be tramping the streets, sleeping where he could. Three meals a day—four, if he wanted them—and a bed in a room all to himself instead of being one in a row of ten, was heaven to him. What the Captain, or the Engineer, or the crew, or anybody else did, was of no moment, so he got back alive. As to the widow's children, he had tried to pick up an acquaintance with them himself— especially the boy—but she had taken them away when she saw how shabby were his clothes.

The Texas Cattle Agent now spoke up. He was a tall, raw-boned man, with a red chin-whisker and red, weather-scorched face, whose clothing looked as if it had been pulled out of shape in the effort to accommodate itself to the spread of his shoulders and round of his thighs. His trousers were tucked in his boots, the straps hanging loose. He generally sat by himself in one corner of the cramped smoking-room, and seldom took part in the conversation. The Bum Actor and he had exchanged confidences the night before, and the Texan therefore felt justified in answering in his friend's stead.

"You're way off, friend," he said to the Man-Who-Knew-It-All. "There ain't nothin' the matter with the Line, nor the ship, nor the Captain. This is my sixth trip aboard of her, and I know! They had a strike among the steve-dores the day we sailed, and then, too, we've got a scrub lot of stokers below, and the Captain's got to handle 'em just so. That kind gets ugly when anything happens. I had sixty head of cattle aboard here on my last trip over, and some of 'em got loose in a storm, and there was hell to pay with the crew till things got straight-ened out. I ain't much on shootin' irons, but they came handy that time. I helped and I know. Got a couple in my cabin now. Needn't tell me nothin' about the Captain. He's all there when he's wanted, and it don't take him more'n a minute, either, to get busy."

The door of the smoking-room opened and the object of his eulogy strolled in. He was evi-dently just off the bridge, for the thrash of the spray still glistened on his oilskins and on his gray, half-moon whiskers. That his word was law aboard ship, and that he enforced it in the fewest words possible, was evident in every line of his face and every tone of his voice. If he deserved an overhauling it certainly would not come from any one on board—least of all from Carhart—the Man-Who-Knew-It-All,

Loosening the thong that bound his so'wester to his chin, he slapped it twice across a chair back, the water flying in every direction, and then faced the room.

"Mr. Bonner."

"Yes, sir," answered the big-shouldered Texan, rising to his feet.

"I'd like to see you for a minute," and without another word the two men left the room and made their way in silence down the wet deck to where the Chief Engineer stood.

"Mike, this is Mr. Bonner; you remember him, don't you? You can rely on his carrying out any orders you give him. If you need another man let him pick him out—" and he continued on to his cabin.

Once there the Captain closed the door behind him, shutting out the pound and swash of the sea; took from a rack over his bunk a roll of charts, spread one on a table and with his head in his hands studied it carefully. The door opened and the Chief Engineer again stood beside him. The Captain raised his head.

"Will Bonner serve?" he asked.

"Yes, glad to, and he thinks he's got another man. He's what he calls out his way a 'tenderfoot,' he says, but he's game and can be depended on. Have you made up your mind where she'll cross?"—and he bent over the chart.

THE THRASH OF THE SPRAY STILL GLISTENED ON HIS OIL SKINS.

The Captain picked up a pair of compasses, balanced them for a moment in his fingers, and with the precision of a seamstress threading a needle, dropped the points astride a wavy line known as the steamer track.

The engineer nodded:

"That will give us about twenty-two hours leeway," he said gravely, "if we make twelve knots."

"Yes, if you make twelve knots: can you do it?"

"I can't say; depends on that gang of shovellers and the way they behave. They're a tough lot—jail-birds and tramps, most of 'em. If they get ugly there ain't but one thing left; that, I suppose, you won't object to."

The Captain paused for a moment in deep thought, glanced at the pin prick in the chart, and said with a certain forceful meaning in his voice:

"No—not if there's no other way."

The Chief Engineer waited, as if for further reply, replaced his cap, and stepped out into the wind. He had got what he came for, and he had got it straight.

With the closing of the door the Captain rolled up the chart, laid it in its place among the others, readjusted the thong of his so'wester, stopped for a moment before a photograph of his wife and child, looked at it long and earnestly, and then mounted the stairs to the bridge. With the exception that the line of his mouth had straightened and the knots in his eyebrows tightened, he was, despite the smoking-room critics, the same bluff, determined sea-dog who had defied the Manager the week before.

II

WHEN Bonner, half an hour later, returned to the smoking-room (he, too, had caught the splash of the sea, the spray drenching the rail), the Bum Actor crossed over and took the seat beside him. The Texan was the only passenger who had spoken to him since he came aboard, and he had already begun to feel lonely. This time he started the conversation by brushing the salt spray from the Agent's coat.

"Got wet, didn't you? Too bad! Wait till I wipe it off," and he dragged a week-old handkerchief from his pocket. Then seeing that the Texan took no notice of the attention, he added, "What did the Captain want?"

The Texan did not reply. He was evidently absorbed in something outside his immediate surroundings, for he continued to sit with bent back, his elbows on his knees, his eyes on the floor.

90

Again the question was repeated:

"What did the Captain want? Nothing the matter, is there?" Fear had always been his master—fear of poverty mostly—and it was poverty in the worst form to others if he failed to get home. This thought had haunted him night and day.

"Yes and no. Don't worry—it'll all come out right. You seem nervous."

"I am. I've been through a lot and have almost reached the end of my rope. Have you got a wife at home?" The Texan shook his head. "Well, if you had you'd understand better than I can tell you. I have, and a three-year-old boy besides. I'd never have left them if I'd known. I came over under contract for a six months' engagement and we were stranded in Pittsburg and had hard work getting back to New York. Some of them are there yet. All I want now is to get home—nothing else will save them. Here's a letter from her I don't mind showing you—you can see for yourself what I'm up against. The boy never was strong."

The big Texan read it through carefully, handed it back without a comment or word of sympathy, and then, with a glance around him, as if in fear of being overheard, asked:

"Can you keep your nerve in a mix-up?"

91

"Do you mean a fight?" queried the Actor.

"Maybe."

"I don't like fights—never did." Anything that would imperil his safe return was to be avoided.

"I neither—but sometimes you've got to. Are you handy with a gun?"

"Why?"

"Nothing—I'm only asking."

Carhart, the Man-Who-Knew-It-All, here lounged over from his seat by the table and dropped into a chair beside them, cutting short his reply. The Texan gave a significant look at the Actor, enforcing his silence, and then buried his face in a newspaper a month old.

Carhart spread his legs, tilted his head back on the chair, slanted his stiff-brim hat until it made a thatch for his nose, and began one of his customary growls: to the room—to the drenched port-holes—to the brim of his hat; as a half-asleep dog sometimes does when things have gone wrong with him—or he dreams they have.

"This ship reminds me of another old tramp, the *Persia*," he drawled. "Same scrub crew and same cut of a Captain. Hadn't been for two of the passengers and me, we'd never got anywhere. Had a fire in the lower hold in a lot of turpentine, and when they put that out we

92

found her cargo had shifted and she was down by the head about six feet. Then the crew made a rush for the boats and left us with only four leaky ones to go a thousand miles. They'd taken 'em all, hadn't been for me and another fellow who stood over them with a gun.''

The Bum Actor raised his eyes.

"What happened then?" he asked in a nervous voice.

"Oh, we pitched in and righted things and got into port at last. But the Captain was no good; he'd a-left with the crew if we'd let him.''

"Is the shifting of a cargo a serious matter?" continued the Actor. "This is my second crossing and I'm not much up on such things.''

"Depends on the weather," interpolated a passenger.

" And on how she's stowed," continued Carhart. "I've been mistrusting this ship ain't plumb on her keel. You can tell that from the way she falls off after each wave strikes her. I have been out on deck looking things over and she seems to me to be down by the stern more than she ought.''

" Maybe she'll be lighter when more coal gets out of her," suggested another passenger.

"Yes, but she's listed some to starboard. I watched her awhile this morning. She ain't

loaded right, or she's loaded *wrong, a-purpose.*
That occurs sometimes with a gang of striking
stevedores.''

The noon whistle blew and the talk ended
with the setting of everybody's watch, except
the Bum Actor's, whose timepiece decorated a
shop-window in the Bowery.

That night one of those uncomfortable rumors,
started doubtless by Carhart's talk, shivered
through the ship, its vibrations even reaching
the widow lying awake in her cabin. This said
that some hundreds of barrels of turpentine had
broken loose and were smashing everything
below. If any one of them rolled into the fur-
naces an explosion would follow which would
send them all to eternity. That this absurdity
was immediately denied by the purser, who asserted with some vehemence that there was not
a gallon of turpentine aboard, did not wholly
allay the excitement, nor did it stifle the nervous
anxiety which had now taken possession of the
passengers.

As the day wore on several additional rumors
joined those already extant. One was dropped
in the ear of the Texan by the Bum Actor as the
two stood on the upper deck watching the sea,
which was rapidly falling.

94

"I got so worried I thought I'd go down into the engine room myself," he whispered. "I'm just back. Something's wrong down there, or I'm mistaken. I wish you'd go and find out. I knew that turpentine yarn was a lie, but I wanted to be sure, so I thought I'd ask one of the stokers who had come up for a little air. He was about to answer me when the Chief Engineer came down from the bridge, where he had been talking to the Captain, and ordered the man below before he had time to fill his lungs. I waited a little while, hoping he or some of the crew would come up again, and then I went down the ladder myself. When I got to the first landing I came bump up against the Chief Engineer. He was standing in the gangway fooling with a revolver he had in his hand as if he'd been cleaning it. 'I'll have to ask you to get back where you came from,' he said. 'This ain't no place for passengers'—and up I came. What do you think it means? I'd get ugly, too, if he kept me in that heat and never let me get a whiff of air. I tell you, that's an awful place down there. Suppose you go and take a look. Your knowing the Captain might make some difference."

"Were any of the stokers around?"

"No—none of them. I didn't see a soul but

95

the Chief Engineer, and I didn't see him more than a minute."

The big Texan moved closer to the rail and again scrutinized the sky-line. He had kept this up all the morning, his eye searching the horizon as he moved from one side of the ship to the other. The inspection over, he slipped his arm through the Actor's and started him down the deck toward the Cattle Agent's cabin. When the two emerged the Texan's face still wore the look which had rested on it since the time the Captain had called him from the smoking-room. The Actor's countenance, however, had undergone a change. All his nervous timidity was gone; his lips were tightly drawn, the line of the jaw more determined. He looked like a man who had heard some news which had first steadied and then solidified him. These changes often overtake men of sensitive, highly strung natures.

On the way back they encountered the Captain accompanied by the Chief Engineer. The two were heading for the saloon, the bugle having sounded for luncheon. As they passed by with their easy, swinging gait, the passengers watched them closely. If there was danger in the air these two officers, of all men, would know it. The Captain greeted the Texan with

96

a significant look, waited until the Actor had been presented, looked the Texan's friend over from head to foot, and then with a nod to several of the others halted opposite a steamer chair in which sat the widow and her two children — one a baby and the other a boy of four — a plump, hugable little fellow, every inch of whose surface invited a caress.

"Please stay a minute and let me talk to you, Captain," the widow pleaded. "I've been so worried. None of these stories are true, are they? There can't be any danger or you would have told me — wouldn't you?"

The Captain laughed heartily, so heartily that even the Chief Engineer looked at him in astonishment. "What stories do you hear, my dear lady?"

"That the steamer isn't loaded properly?"

Again the Captain laughed, this time under the curls of the chubby boy whom he had caught in his arms and was kissing eagerly.

"Not loaded right?" he puffed at last when he got his breath. "Well, well, what a pity! That yarn, I guess, comes from some of the navigators in the smoking-room. They generally run the ship. Here, you little rascal, turn out your toes and dance a jig for me. No — no — not that way — this way — out with them! Here,

97

let me show you. One — two — off we go. Now the pigeon wing and the double twist and the rat-tat-tat, rat-tat-tat—that's the way, my lad!"

He had the boy's hands now, the child shouting with laughter, the overjoyed mother clapping her hands as the big burly Captain with his face twice as red from the exercise, danced back and forth across the deck, the passengers forming a ring about them.

"There!" sputtered the Captain, all out of breath from the exercise, as he dropped the child back into the widow's arms. "Now all of you come down to luncheon. The weather is getting better every minute. The glass is rising and we are going to have a fine night."

Carhart, who had watched the whole performance with an ill-concealed sneer on his face, muttered to the man next him:

"What did I tell you? He's a pretty kind of a Captain, ain't he? He's mashed on the widow just as I told you. Smoking-room yarn, is it? I bet I could pick out half a dozen men right in them chairs who could run the ship as well as he does. Maybe we'll have to take charge, after all—don't you think so, Mr. Bonner?"

The Texan smiled grimly: "I'll let you do the picking, Mr. Carhart—" and with his hand on the Actor's arm, the two went below.

A counter-current now swept through the ship. If anything was really the matter the Captain would not be dancing jigs, nor would he leave the bridge for his meals. This, like all other counter-currents — wave or otherwise — tossed up a bobble of dispute when the two clashed. There was no doubt about it: Carhart had been "talking through his hat" — "shooting off his mouth" — the man was "a gas bag," etc., etc. When appeal for confirmation was made to the Texan and the Actor, who now seemed inseparable, neither made reply. They evidently did not care to be mixed up in what Bonner characterized with a grim smile as "more hot air."

All through the meal the Captain kept up his good-natured mood; chatting with the widow who sat on his right, the baby in her lap; making a pig of a lemon and some tooth-picks for the boy, who had crawled up into his arms; exchanging nods and smiles down the length of the table with several new arrivals, or congratulating those nearest to him on their recovery after the storm, ending by carrying both boy and baby to the upper deck — so that he might "not forget how to handle" his own when he got back, he laughed in explanation.

III

LUNCHEON over, the passengers, many of whom had been continuously in their berths, began to crowd the decks. These soon discovered that the ship was not on an even keel; a fact confirmed when attention was called to the slant of the steamer chairs and the roll of an orange toward the scuppers. Explanation was offered by the Texan, who argued that the wind had hauled, and being then abeam had given her a list to starboard. This, while not wholly satisfactory to the more experienced, allayed the fears of the women — there were two or three on board beside the widow — who welcomed the respite from the wrench and stagger of the previous hours.

Attention was now drawn by a nervous passenger to a gang of sailors under the First Officer, who were at work overhauling the boats on the forward deck, immediately under the eyes of the Captain who had returned to the bridge, as well as to an approaching wall of fog which, while he was speaking, had blanketed the ship, sending two of the boat gang on a run to the bow. The fog-horn also blew continuously, almost without intermission. Now and then it would give three short, sharp snorts, as if of warning.

The passengers had now massed themselves in groups, some touch of sympathy, or previous acquaintance, or trait of courage but recently discovered, having drawn them together. Again the Captain passed down the deck. This time he stopped to light a cigarette from a passenger's cigar, remarking as he did so that it was "as thick as pea soup on the bridge, but he thought it would lighten before morning." Then halting beside the chair of an old lady who had but recently appeared on deck, he congratulated her on her recovery and kept on his way to the boats.

The widow, however, was still anxious.

"What are they doing with the boats?" she asked, her eyes following the Captain's disappearing figure.

"Only overhauling them, madam," spoke up the Texan, who had stationed himself near her chair.

"But isn't that unusual?" she inquired in a tremulous voice.

"No, madam, just precaution, and always a safe one in a fog. Collision comes so quick sometimes they don't have time even to clear the davits."

"But the sailors are carrying up boxes and

kegs and putting them in the boats; what's that for?" broke in another passenger, who had been leaning over the forward rail.

"Grub and water, I guess," returned the Texan. "It's a thousand miles to the nearest land, and there ain't no bakery on the way that I know of. Can't be too careful when there's women and babies aboard, especially little fellows like these—" and he ran his hand through the boy's curls. "The Captain don't take no chances. That's what I like him for."

Again the current of hope submerged the current of despair. The slant of the deck, however, increased, although the wind had gone down; so much so that the steamer chairs had to be lashed to the iron hand-hold skirting the wall of the upper cabins. So had the fog, which was now so dense that it hid completely the work of the boat gang.

With the passing of the afternoon and the approach of night, thus deepening the gloom, there was added another and a new anxiety to the drone of the fog-horn. This was a Coston signal which flashed from the bridge, flooding the deck with light and pencilling masts and rigging in lines of fire. These flashes kept up at intervals of five minutes, the colors changing from time to time.

An indefinable fear now swept through the vessel. The doubters and scoffers from the smoking-room who stood huddled together near the forward companion-way talked in whispers. The slant of the deck they argued might be due to a shift of the cargo—a situation serious, but not dangerous—but why burn Costons? The only men who seemed to be holding their own, and who were still calm and undisturbed, were the Texan and the Actor. These, during the conference, had moved toward the flight of steps leading to the bridge and had taken their positions near the bottom step, but within reach of the widow's chair. Once the Actor loosened his coat and slipped in his hand as if to be sure of something he did not want to lose.

While this was going on the Captain left the bridge in charge of the Second Officer and descended to his cabin. Reaching over his bunk, he unhooked the picture of his wife and child, tore it from its frame, looked at it intently for a moment, and then, with a sigh, slid it into an inside pocket. This done, he stripped off his wet storm coat, thrust his arms into a close-fitting reefing jacket, unhooked a holster from its place, dropped its contents into his outside pocket, and walked slowly down the flight of steps to where the Texan and the Actor stood waiting.

Then, facing the passengers, and in the same tone of voice with which he would have ordered a cup of coffee from a steward, he said:

"My friends, I find it necessary to abandon the ship. There is time enough and no necessity for crowding. The boats are provisioned for thirty days. The women and children will go first: this order will be literally carried out; those who disobey it will have to be dealt with in another way. This, I hope, you will not make necessary. I will also tell you that I believe we are still within the steamer zone, although the fog and weather have prevented any observation. Do you stay here, madam. I'll come for you when I am ready —" and he laid his hand encouragingly on the widow's arm.

With this he turned to the Texan and the Actor:

"You understand, both of you, do you not, Mr. Bonner? You and your friend will guard the aft companion-way, and help the Chief Engineer take care of the stokers and the steerage. I and the First Officer will fill the boats."

The beginning of a panic is like the beginning of a fire: first a curl of smoke licking through a closed sash, then a rush of flame, and then a roar freighted with death. Its subduing is along similar lines: A sharp command clearing the way, concentrated effort, and courage.

Here the curl of smoke was an agonized shriek from an elderly woman who fell fainting on the deck; the rush of flame was a wild surge of men hurling themselves toward the boats, and the roar which meant death was the frenzied throng of begrimed half-naked stokers and crazed emigrants who were wedged in a solid mass in the companion-way leading to the upper deck. The subduing was the same.

"Back, all of you!" shouted the Engineer. "The first man who passes that door without my permission I'll kill! Five of you at a time — no crowding — keep 'em in line, Mr. Bonner — you and your friend!"

The Texan and the Bum Actor were within three feet of him as he spoke — the Texan as cool as if he were keeping count of a drove of steers, except that he tallied with the barrel of a six-shooter instead of a note-book and pencil. The Bum Actor's face was deathly white and his pistol hand trembled a little, but he did not flinch. He ranged the lucky ones in line farther along, and kept them there. "Anything to get home," he had told the Texan when he had slipped Bonner's other revolver, an hour before, into his pocket.

On the saloon deck the flame of fear was still raging, although the sailors and the three stewards were so many moving automatons under the First Officer's orders. The widow, with her baby held tight to her breast, had not moved from where the Captain had placed her, nor had she uttered a moan. The crisis was too great for anything but implicit obedience. The Captain had kept his word, and had told her when danger threatened ; she must now wait for what God had in store for her. The boy stood by the First Officer; he had clapped his hands and laughed when he saw the first boat swung clear of the davits.

Carhart was the color of ashes and could hardly articulate. He had edged up close to the gangway where the boats were to be filled. Twice he had tried to wedge himself between the First Officer and the rail and twice had been pushed back — the last time with a swing that landed him against a pile of steamer chairs.

All this time the fog-horn had kept up its monotonous din, the Costons flaring at intervals. The stoppage of either would only have added to the terror now partly allayed by the Captain's encouraging talk, which was picked up and repeated all over the ship.

"BACK, ALL OF YOU!" SHOUTED THE ENGINEER. "THE FIRST MAN
WHO PASSES THAT DOOR WITHOUT MY PERMISSION, I'LL KILL!"

The first boat was now ready for passengers.

"This way, madam—you first—" the Captain said to the widow. "You must go alone with the baby, and I—"

He did not finish the sentence. Something had caught his ear—something that made him lunge heavily toward the rail, his eyes searching the gloom, his hand cupped to his ear.

"Hold hard, men!" he cried. "Keep still— all of you!"

Out of the stillness of the night came the moan of a distant fog-horn. This was followed by a wild cheer from the men at the boat davits. At the same instant a dim, far-away light cut its way through the black void, burned for a moment, and disappeared like a dying star.

Another cheer went up. This time the watch on the foretop and the men astride the nose sent it whirling through the choke and damp with an added note of joy.

The Captain turned to the widow.

"That's her—that's the *St. Louis!* I've been hoping for her all day, and didn't give up until the fog shut in."

"And we can stay here!"

"No—we haven't a moment to lose. Our fires are nearly out now. We've been in a sinking condition for forty-eight hours. We sprung a leak where we couldn't get at it, and our pumps are clogged.

"Stand aside, men! All ready, madam! No, you can't manage them both — give me the boy, — I'll bring him in the last boat."

THE LITTLE GRAY LADY

I

ONCE in a while there come to me out of the long ago the fragments of a story I have not thought of for years—one that has been hidden in the dim lumber-room of my brain where I store my by-gone memories.

These fragments thrust themselves out of the past as do the cuffs of an old-fashioned coat, the flutings of a flounce, or the lacings of a bodice from out a quickly opened bureau drawer. Only when you follow the cuff along the sleeve to the broad shoulder; smooth out the crushed frill that swayed about her form, and trace the silken thread to the waist it tightened, can you determine the fashion of the day in which they were worn.

And with the rummaging of this lumber-room come the odors: dry smells from musty old trunks packed with bundles of faded letters and worthless deeds tied with red tape; musty smells from dust-covered chests, iron bound,

109

holding mouldy books, their backs loose; pungent smells from cracked wardrobes stuffed with moth-eaten hunting-coats, riding-trousers, and high boots with rusty spurs — cross-country riders these — roisterers and gamesters—a sorry lot, no doubt.

Or perhaps it is an old bow-legged high-boy — its club-feet slippered on easy rollers—the kind with deep drawers kept awake by rattling brass handles, its outside veneer so highly polished that you are quite sure it must have been brought up in some distinguished family. The scent of old lavender and spiced rose leaves, and a stick or two of white orris root, haunt this relic: my lady's laces must be kept fresh, and so must my lady's long white mitts — they reach from her dainty knuckles quite to her elbow. And so must her cobwebbed silk stockings and the filmy kerchief she folds across her bosom.

It is this kind of a drawer that I am opening now — one belonging to the Little Gray Lady.

As I look through its contents my eyes resting on the finger of a glove, the end of a lace scarf, and the handle of an old fan, my mind goes back to the last time she wore them. Then I begin turning everything upside down, lifting the corner of this incident, prying under that bit of talk, recalling what he said and who told of it (I shall have the whole drawer empty before I get through), and whose fault it was that the match was broken off, and why she, of all women in the world, should have remained single all those years. Why, too, she should have lost her identity, so to speak, and become the Little Gray Lady.

And yet no sobriquet could better express her personality : She was little—a dainty, elf-like littleness, with tiny feet and wee hands; she was gray—a soft, silver gray—too gray for her forty years (and this fragment begins when she was forty); and she was a lady in every beat of her warm heart; in every pressure of her white hand; in her voice, speech—in all her thoughts and movements.

She lived in the quaintest of old houses fronted by a brick path bordered with fragrant box, which led up to an old-fashioned porch, its door brightened by a brass knocker. This, together with the knobs, steps, and slits of windows on each side of the door, was kept scrupulously clean by old Margaret, who had lived with her for years.

But it is her personality and not her surroundings that lingers in my memory. No one ever heard anything sweeter than her voice;

and nobody ever looked into a lovelier face, even
if there were little hollows in the cheeks and
shy, fanlike wrinkles lurking about the corners
of her lambent brown eyes. Nor did her gray
hair mar her beauty. It was not old, dry, and
withered — a wispy gray. (That is not the way
it happened.) It was a new, all-of-a-sudden
gray, and in less than a week — so Margaret
once told me — bleaching its brown gold to
silver. But the gloss remained, and so did the
richness of the folds, and the wealth and weight
of it.

Inside the green-painted door, with its white
trim and brass knocker and knobs, there was a
narrow hall hung with old portraits, opening into
a room literally all fireplace. Here there were
gouty sofas, and five or six big easy-chairs
ranged in a half-circle, with arms held out as if
begging somebody to sit in them; and here, too,
was an embroidered worsted fire screen that slid
up and down a standard, to shield one's face
from the blazing logs; and there were queer
tables and old-gold curtains looped back with
brass rosettes — ears really — behind which the
tresses of the parted curtains were tucked; and
there were more old portraits in dingy frames,
and samplers under glass, and a rug which some
aunt had made with her own hands from odds

and ends; and a huge work-basket spilling wors-
teds, and last, and by no manner of means
least, a big chintz-covered rocking-chair, the
little lady's very own—its thin ankles and splay
feet hidden by a modest frill. There were all
these things and a lot more—and yet I still main-
tain that the room was just one big fireplace.
Not alone because of its size (and it certainly was
big: many a doubting curly head, losing its
faith in Santa Claus, has crawled behind the
old fire-dogs, the child's fingers tight about the
Little Gray Lady's, and been told to look up
into the blue—a lesson never forgotten all their
lives), but because of the wonderful and never-
to-be-told-of things which constantly took place
before its blazing embers.

For this fireplace was the Little Gray Lady's
altar. Here she dispensed wisdom and cheer
and love. Everybody in Pomford village had
sat in one or the other of the chairs grouped
about it and had poured out their hearts to her.
All sorts of pourings: love affairs, for instance,
that were hopeless until she would take the girl's
hand in her own and smooth out the tangle; to
say nothing of bickerings behind closed doors,
with two lives pulling apart until her dear arms
brought them together.

But all this is only the outside of the old mahogany high-boy with its meerschaum-pipe polish, spraddling legs, and rattling handles.

Now for the Little Gray Lady's own particular drawer.

II

It was Christmas Eve, and Kate Dayton, one of Pomford's pretty girls, had found the Little Gray Lady sitting alone before the fire gazing into the ashes, her small frame almost hidden in the roomy chair. The winter twilight had long since settled and only the flickering blaze of the logs and the dim glow from one lone candle illumined the room. This, strange to say, was placed on a table in a corner where its rays shed but little light in the room.

"Oh! Cousin Annie," moaned Kate (everybody in Pomford who got close enough to touch the Little Gray Lady's hand called her "Cousin Annie"—it was only the outside world who knew her by her other sobriquet), "I didn't mean anything. Mark came in just at the wrong minute, and—and—" The poor girl's tears smothered the rest.

"Don't let him go, dearie," came the answer, when she had heard the whole story, the girl on her knees, her head in her lap, the wee

114

hand stroking the fluff of golden hair dishevelled in her grief.

"Oh, but he won't stay!" moaned Kate. "He says he is going to Rio—way out to South America to join his Uncle Harry."

"He won't go, dearie—not if you tell him the truth and make him tell you the truth. Don't let your pride come in; don't beat around the bush or make believe you are hurt or misunderstood, or that you don't care. You do care. Better be a little humble now than humble all your life. It only takes a word. Hold out your hand and say: 'I'm sorry, Mark—please forgive me.' If he loves you—and he does—"

The girl raised her head: "Oh! Cousin Annie! How do you know?"

She laughed gently. "Because he was here, dearie, half an hour ago and told me so. He thought you owed him the dance, and he was a little jealous of Tom."

"But Tom had asked me—"

"Yes—and so had Mark—"

"Yes—but he had no right—" She was up in arms again: she wouldn't—she couldn't—and again an outburst of tears choked her words.

The Little Gray Lady had known Kate's mother, now dead, and what might have hap-

pened but for a timely word—and she knew
to her own sorrow what had happened for want
of one. Kate and Mark should not repeat that
experience if she could help it. She had saved
the mother in the old days by just such a word.
She would save the daughter in the same way.
And the two were much alike—same slight, girlish
figure; same blond hair and blue eyes; same
expression, and the same impetuous, high-strung
temperament. "If that child's own mother
walked in this minute I couldn't tell 'em apart,
they do favor one another so," old Margaret had
told her mistress when she opened the door for
the girl, and she was right. Pomford village was
full of these hereditary likenesses. Mark Dabney, whom all the present trouble was about, was
so like his father at his age that his Uncle Harry
had picked Mark out on a crowded dock when
the lad had visited him in Rio the year before, although he had not seen the boy's father for twenty years—so strong was the family likeness.

If there was to be a quarrel it must not be between the Dabneys and the Daytons, of all
families. There had been suffering enough in
the old days.

"Listen, dearie," she said in her gentle, crooning tone, patting the girl's cheek as she talked.
"A quarrel where there is no love is soon for-

gotten, but a difference when both love may, if not quickly healed, leave a scar that will last through life.''

''There are as good fish in the sea as were ever caught,'' cried the girl in sheer bravado, brushing away her tears.

''Don't believe it, dearie—and don't ever say it. That has wrecked more lives than you know. That is what I once knew a girl to say—a girl just about your age—''

''But she found somebody else, and that's just what I'm going to do. I'm not going to have Mark read me a lecture every time I want to do something he doesn't like. Didn't your girl find somebody else?''

'' No—never. She is still unmarried.''

''Yes—but it wasn't her fault, was it?''

''Yes—although she did not know it at the time. She opened a door suddenly and found her lover alone with another girl. The two had stolen off together where they would not be interrupted. He was pleading for his college friend—straightening out just some such foolish quarrel as you have had with Mark—but the girl would not understand; nor did she know the truth until a year afterward. Then it was too late.''

The Little Gray Lady stopped, lifted her hand

from the girl's head, and turned her face toward the now dying fire.

" And what became of him ? " asked the girl in a hushed voice, as if she dared not awaken the memory.

" He went away and she has never seen him since."

For some minutes there was silence, then Kate said in a braver tone:

"And he married somebody else ? "

"No."

"Well, then, she died ? "

"No."

The Littie Lady had not moved, nor had she taken her eyes from the blaze. She seemed to be addressing some invisible body who could hear and understand. The girl felt its influence and a tremor ran through her. The fitful blaze casting weird shadows helped this feeling. At last, with an effort, she asked:

"You say you know them both, Cousin Annie ? "

" Yes—he was my dear friend. I was just thinking of him when you came in."

The charred logs broke into a heap of coals; the blaze flickered and died. But for the lone candle in the corner the room would have been in total darkness.

"Shall I light another candle, Cousin Annie?" shivered the girl, "or bring that one nearer?"

"No, it's Christmas Eve, and I only light one candle on Christmas Eve."

"But what's one candle! Why, father has the whole house as bright as day and every fire blazing." The girl sprang to her feet and stepped nearer the hearth. She would be less nervous, she thought, if she moved about, and then the warmth of the fire was somehow reassuring. "Please let me light them all, Cousin Annie," she pleaded, reaching out her hand toward a cluster in an old-fashioned candelabra — "and if there aren't enough I'll get more from Margaret."

"No, no—one will do. It is an old custom of mine; I've done it for twenty years."

"But don't you love Christmas?" Kate argued, her nervousness increasing. The ghostly light and the note of pain in her companion's voice were strangely affecting.

The Little Gray Lady leaned forward in her chair and looked long and steadily at the heap of smouldering ashes; then she answered slowly, each word vibrating with the memory of some hidden sorrow: "I've had mine, dearie."

"But you can have some more," urged Kate.

"Not like those that have gone before, dearie —no, not like those."

Something in the tones of her voice and quick droop of the dear head stirred the girl to her depths. Sinking to her knees she hid her face in the Little Lady's lap.

"And you sit here in the dark with only one candle?" she whispered.

"Yes, always," she answered, her fingers stroking the fair hair. "I can see those I have loved better in the dark. Sometimes the room is full of people; I have often to strain my eyes to assure myself that the door is really shut. All sorts of people come — the girls and boys I knew when I was young. Some are dead; some are far away; some so near that should I open the window and shout their names many of them could hear. There are fewer above ground every year — but I welcome all who come. It's the old maid's hour, you know—this twilight hour. The wives are making ready the supper; the children are romping; lovers are together in the corner where they can whisper and not be overheard. But none of this disturbs me—no big man bursts in, letting in the cold. I have my chair, my candle, my thoughts, and my fire. When you get to be my age, Kate, and live alone—and you might, dearie, if Mark should leave you — you will love these twilight hours, too."

The girl reached up her hands and touched the Little Gray Lady's cheek, whispering:

"But aren't you very, *very* lonely, Cousin Annie?"

"Yes, sometimes."

For a moment Kate remained silent, then she asked in a faltering voice through which ran a note almost of terror:

"Do you think I shall ever be like — like — that is — I shall ever be — all alone?"

"I don't know, dearie. No one can ever tell what will happen. I never thought twenty years ago I should be all alone — but I am."

The girl raised her head, and with a cry of pain threw her arms around the Little Gray Lady's neck:

"Oh, no! — no! I can't bear it!" she sobbed! "I'll tell Mark! I'll send for him — to-night — before I go to bed!"

III

It was not until Kate Dayton reached her father's gate that the spell wrought by the flickering firelight and the dim glow of the ghostly candle wore off. The crisp air of the winter night—for it was now quite dark—had helped, but the sight of Mark's waiting figure striding along the snow-covered path to her home, and his manly, outspoken apology, "Please forgive me, Kate, I made an awful fool of myself," followed by her joyous refrain, "Oh, Mark! I've been so wretched!" had done more. It had all come just as Cousin Annie had said; there had been neither pride nor anger. Only the Little Gray Lady's timely word.

But if the spell was broken the pathetic figure of the dear woman, her eyes fixed on the dying embers, still lingered in Kate's mind.

"Oh, Mark, it is so pitiful to see her!—and I got so frightened; the whole room seemed filled with ghosts. Christmas seems her loneliest time. She won't have but one candle lighted, and she sits and mopes in the dark. Oh, it's dreadful! I tried to cheer her up, but she says she likes to sit in the dark, because then all the dead people she loves can come to her. Can't we do something to make her happy? She is so lovely, and she is so little, and she is so dear!"

They had entered the house, now a blaze of light. Kate's father was standing on the hearth rug, his back to a great fireplace filled with roaring logs.

"Where have you two gadabouts been?" he

laughed merrily. "What do you mean by stay-
ing out this late? Don't you know it's Christmas Eve?"

"We've been to see Cousin Annie, daddy;
and it would make your heart ache to look at
her! She's there all alone. Can't you go down
and bring her up here?"

"Yes, I could, but she wouldn't come, not on
Christmas Eve. Did she have her candle burning?"

"Yes, just one poor little miserable candle
that hardly gave any light at all."

"And it was in the corner on a little table?"

"Yes, all by itself."

"Poor dear, she always lights it. She's lighted
it for almost twenty years."

"Is it for somebody she loved who died?"

"No—it's for somebody she loved who is
alive, but who never came back and won't."

He studied them both for a moment, as if in
doubt, then he added in a determined voice,
motioning them to a seat beside him:

"It is about time you two children heard the
story straight, for it concerns you both, so I'll
tell you. Your Uncle Harry, Mark, is the man
who never came back and won't. He was
just your age at the time. He and Annie were
to be married in a few months, then everything

123

went to smash. And it was your mother, Kate, who was the innocent cause of his exile. Harry, who was the best friend I had in the world, tried to put in a good word for me—this was before I and your mother were engaged—and Annie, coming in and finding them, got it all crooked. Instead of waiting until Harry could explain, she flared up, and off he went. Her hair turned white in a week when she found out how she had misjudged him, but it was too late then— Harry wouldn't come back, and he never will. When he told you, Mark, last year in Rio that he was coming home Christmas I knew he'd change his mind just as soon as you left him, and he did. Queer boy, Harry. Once he gets an idea in his head it sticks there. He was that way when he was a boy. He'll never come back as long as Annie lives, and that means never.''

He stopped a moment, spread his fingers to the blazing logs, and then, with a smile on his face, said: ''If ever I catch you two young turtle-doves making such fools of yourselves, I'll turn you both out doors,'' and again his hearty laugh rang through the cheery room.

The girl instinctively leaned closer to her lover. She had heard some part of the story before—in fact, both of them had, but never in its entirety. Her heart went out to the Little Gray Lady all the more.

Mark now spoke up. He, too, had had an hour of his own with the Little Gray Lady, and the obligation still remained unsettled.

"Well, if she won't come up here and have Christmas with us," he cried, "why can't we go down there and have Christmas with her? Let's surprise her, Kate; let's clean out all those dead people. I know she sits in the dark and imagines they all come back, for I've seen her that way many a time when I drop in on her in the late afternoon. Let's show her they're alive."

Kate started up and caught Mark's arm. "Oh, Mark! I have it!" she whispered, "and we will—yes—that will be the very thing," and so with more mumblings and mutterings, not one word of which could her father hear, the two raced up-stairs to the top of the house and the garret.

IV

Two hours later a group of young people led by Mark Dabney trooped out of Kate's gate and turned down the Little Gray Lady's street. Most of them wore long cloaks and were muffled in thick veils.

They were talking in low tones, glancing from side to side, as if fearing to be seen. The moon had gone under a cloud, but the light of the stars, aided by an isolated street lamp, showed them the way. So careful were they to conceal their identity that the whole party — there were six in all — would dart into an open gate, crouching behind the snow-laden hedge to avoid even a single passer-by. Only once were they in any danger, and that was when a sleigh gliding by stopped in front of them, the driver calling out in a voice which sounded twice as loud in the white stillness: "Where's Mr. Dabney's new house?" (evidently a stranger, for the town pump was not better known). No one else stopped them until they reached the Little Gray Lady's porch.

Kate crept up first, followed by Mark, and peered in. So far as she could see everything was just as she had left it.

"The candle is still burning, Mark, and she's put more wood on the fire. But I can't find her. Oh, yes — there she is — in her big chair — you can just see the top of her head and her hand. Hush! don't one of you breathe. Now, listen, girls! Mark and I will tiptoe in first — the front door is never fastened — and if she is asleep — and I think she is — we will all crouch down behind her until she wakes up."

"And another thing," whispered Mark from behind his hand—"everybody must drop their coats and things in the hall, so we can surprise her all at once."

The strange procession tiptoed in and arranged itself behind the Little Gray Lady's chair. Kate was dressed in her mother's wedding-gown, flaring poke bonnet, and long, faded gloves clear to her shoulder; Mark had on a blue coat with brass buttons, a buff waistcoat, and black stock, the two points of the high collar pinching his ruddy cheeks—the same dress his father and Uncle Harry had worn, and all the young bloods of their day, for that matter. The others were in their grandmother's or grandfather's short and long clothes, Tom Fields sporting a tight-sleeved, high-collared coat, silk-embroidered waistcoat, and pumps.

Kate crept up behind her chair, but Mark moved to the fireplace and rested his elbow on the mantel, so that he would be in full view when the Little Gray Lady awoke.

At last her eyes opened, but she made no out-cry, nor did she move, except to lift her head as does a fawn startled by some sudden light, her wondering eyes drinking in the apparition. Mark, hardly breathing, stood like a statue, but Kate, bending closer, heard her catch her breath

127

with a long, indrawn sigh, and next the half-
audible words: "No—it isn't so— How foolish
I am—" Then there came softly: "Harry—"
and again in almost a whisper—as if hope had
died in her heart—"Harry—"

Kate, half frightened, sprang forward and
flung her arms around the Little Gray Lady.

"Why, don't you know him? It's Mark,
Cousin Annie, and here's Tom and Nanny
Fields, and everybody, and we're going to light
all the candles—every one of them, and make an
awful big fire—and have a real, real Christmas."

The Little Gray Lady was awake now.

"Oh! you scared me so!" she cried, rising to
her feet, rubbing her eyes. "You foolish children! I must have been asleep—yes, I know I
was!" She greeted them all, talking and enter-
ing into their fun, the spirit of hospitality now
hers, saying over and over again how glad she
was they came, kissing one and another; telling
them how happy they made her; how since
they had been kind enough to come, she would
let them have a *real* Christmas—"Only," she
added quickly, "it will have to be by the light
of one candle; but that won't make any difference, because you can pile on just as much wood
as you choose. "Yes," she continued, her voice

rising in her effort to meet them on their own joyous plane—"pile on all the kindling, too, Mark; and Kate, dear, please run and tell Margaret to bring in every bit of cake she has in the pantry. Oh, how like your mother you are, Kate! I remember that very dress. And you, Mark! Why, you've got on the same coat I saw your father wear at the Governor's ball. And you, too, Tom. Oh, what a good time we will all have!"

Soon the lid of the old piano was raised, a spinet, really, and one of the girls began running her fingers over the keys; and later on it was agreed that the first dance was to be the Virginia reel, with all the hospitable chairs and the fire screen and the gouty old sofa rolled back against the wall.

This all arranged, Mark took his place with the Little Gray Lady for a partner. The music struck up a lively tune and as quickly ceased as the sound of bells rang through the night air. In the hush that followed a sleigh was heard at the gate.

Kate sprang up and clapped her hands.

"Oh, they are just in time! There come the rest of them, Cousin Annie. Now we are going to have a great party! Let's be dancing when they come in; keep on playing!"

At this instant the door opened and Margaret put in her head. "Somebody," she said, with a low bow, "wants to see Mr. Mark on business."

Mark, looking like a gallant of the old school, excused himself with a great flourish to the Little Gray Lady and strode out. In the hall, with his back to the light, stood a broad-shouldered man muffled to the chin in a fur overcoat. The boy was about to apologize for his costume and then ask the man's errand, when the stranger turned quickly and gripped his wrist.

"Hush—not a word! Where is she?" he cried.

With a low whistle of surprise Mark pushed open the door. The stranger stepped in.

The Little Gray Lady raised her head.

"And who can this new guest be?" she asked—"and in what a queer costume, too!"

The man drew himself up to his full height and threw wide his coat: "And you don't know me, Annie?"

She did not take her eyes from his face, nor did she move except to turn her head appealingly to the room as if she feared they were playing her another trick.

He had reached her side and stood looking down at her. Again came the voice—a strong, clear voice, with a note of infinite tenderness through it:

"How white your hair is, Annie; and your hand is so thin! Have I changed like this?"

She leaned forward, scanning him eagerly.

There was a little cry, then all her soul went out in the one word:

"Harry!"

She was inside the big coat now, his strong arms around her, her head hidden on his breast, only the tips of her toes on the floor.

When he had kissed her again and again— and he did and before everybody—he crossed the room, picked up the ghostly candle, and smothered its flame.

"I saw it from the road," he laughed softly, "that's why I couldn't wait. But you'll never have to light it again, my darling!"

I saw them both a few years later. Everything in the way of fading and wrinkling had stopped so far as the Little Gray Lady was concerned. If there were any lines left in her forehead and around the corners of her eyes, I could not find them. Joy had planted a crop of dimples instead, and they had spread out, smoothing the care lines. Margaret even claimed that her hair was turning brown gold once more,

131

but then Margaret was always her loyal slave, and believed everything her mistress wished.

And now, if you don't mind, dear reader, we will put everything back and shut the Little Gray Lady's bureau drawer.

THE MAN IN THE HIGH-WATER BOOTS

NOW and then in my various prowlings I have met a man with a personality; one with mental equipment, heart endowment, self-forgetfulness, and charm—the kind of charm that makes you glad when he comes and sorry when he goes.

One was a big-chested, straight-backed, clear-eyed, clean-souled sea-dog, with arms of hickory, fingers of steel, and a brain in instant touch with a button marked "Experience and Pluck." Another was a devil-may-care, barefooted Venetian, who wore a Leporello hat canted over one eye and a scarlet sash about his thin, shapely waist, and whose corn teeth gleamed and flashed as he twisted his mustache or threw kisses to the pretty bead-stringers crossing Ponte Lungo. Still a third was a little sawed-off, freckled-faced, red-headed Irishman, who drove a cab through London fogs in winter, poled my punt among the lily-pads in summer, and hung wall-paper between times.

These I knew and *loved;* even now the cockles

of my heart warm up when I think of them. Others I knew and *liked;* the difference being simply one of personality.

This time it is a painter who crosses my path —a mere lad of thirty two or three, all boy— heart, head, and brush. I had caught a glimpse of him in New York, when he "blew in" (no other phrase expresses his movement) where his pictures were being hung, and again in Philadelphia when some crushed ice and a mixture made it pleasant for everybody, but I had never examined all four sides of him until last summer.

We were at Dives at the time, lunching in the open courtyard of the inn, three of us, when the talk drifted toward the young painter, his life at his old mill near Eure and his successes at the Salon and elsewhere. Our host, the Sculptor, had come down in his automobile—a long, low, double-jointed crouching tiger—a forty-devil-power machine, fearing neither God nor man, and which is bound sooner or later to come to an untimely end and the scrap heap.

All about, fringing the tea tables and filling the summer air with their chatter and laughter, were gathered not only the cream, but the very top skimmings of all the fashion and folly of Trouville—twenty minutes away, automobile time—their blossoming hats, full-blown parasols, and pink and white veils adding another flower-bed to the quaint old courtyard.

With the return of the Man from the Latin Quarter, his other guest, who knew the ins and outs of the cellar, and who had gone in search of a certain vintage known only to the initiated (don't forget to ask for it when you go — it has no label, but the cork is sealed with yellow wax; M. Ramois, the good landlord, will know the kind — *if he thinks you do*), our host, the Sculptor, his mind still on his friend the painter, looked up and said, as he reached for the cork-screw :

"Why not go to-morrow? The mill is the most picturesque thing you ever saw — an old Louis XIII house and mill on the River Rille near Beaumont-le-Roger, once inhabited by the poet Chateaubriand. The river runs underground in the sands for some distance and comes out a few miles from Knight's — cold as ice and clear as crystal and packed full of trout. Besides Knight is at home — had a line from him this morning."

The Man from the Quarter laid down his glass.

"How far is it?" This man is so daft on fishing that he has been known to kiss the first trout he hooks in the spring.

"Only fifty-six miles, my dear boy — run you over in an hour."

135

"And everything else that gets in the way," said the Man from the Quarter, moving his glass nearer the Sculptor's elbow.

"No danger of that—I've got a siren that you can hear for a mile — but really, it's only a step."

I once slid down a salt mine on a pair of summer pantaloons and brought up in total darkness (a godsend under the circumstances). I still shudder when I think of the speed; of the way my hair tried to leave my scalp; of the peculiar blink in my eyes; of the hours it took to live through forty seconds; and of my final halt in the middle of a moon-faced, round-paunched German who was paid a mark for saving the bones and necks of idiots like myself.

This time the sliding was done in an overcoat (although the summer sun was blazing), a steamer cap, and a pair of goggles. First there came a shivery chuggetty-chug, as if the beast was shaking himself loose. Next a noise like the opening of a bolt in an iron cage, and then the Inn of William the Conqueror—the village— beach, inlet—wide sea, streamed behind like a panorama run at high pressure.

The first swoop was along the sea, a whirl into Houlgate, a mad dash through the village, dogs and chickens running for dear life, and out

136

again with the deadly rush of a belated wild
goose hurrying to a southern clime. Our host
sat beside the chauffeur, who looked like the
demon in a ballet in his goggles and skull-cap.
The Man from the Quarter and I crouched on
the rear seats, our eyes on the turn of the road
ahead. What we had left behind, or what
might be on either side of us was of no moment;
what would come around that far-distant curve
a mile away and a minute off was what troubled
us. The demon and the Sculptor were as cool
as the captain and first mate on the bridge of a
liner in a gale; the Man from the Quarter
stared doggedly ahead; I was too scared for
scenery and too proud to ask the Sculptor to
slow down, so I thought of my sins and slowly
murmured, "Now I lay me."

When we got to the top of the last hill and had
swirled into the straight broad turnpike leading
to Lisieux, the Sculptor spoke in an undertone
to the demon, did something with his foot or hand
or teeth—everything with which he could push,
pull, or bite was busy—and the machine, as if
struck by a lash, sprang into space. Trees,
fences, little farmhouses, hay-stacks, canvas-
covered wagons, frightened children, dogs, now
went by in blurred outlines; ten miles, thirty
miles, then a string of villages, Liseau among

them, the siren shrieking like a lost soul sinking into perdition.

"Watch the road to the right," wheezed the Sculptor between his breaths; "that is where the Egyptian prince was killed—" this over his shoulder to me—"a tram-car hit him—you can see the hole in the bank. Made that last mile in sixty-five seconds—running fifty-nine now—look out for that cross-road—" Wow-wow-oo—wow-wow (siren). "Damn that market cart —" Wow-wow-o-o-wow. "Slow up, or we'll be on top of that donkey—just grazed it. Can't tell what a donkey will do when a girl's driving it." Wow-oo-w-o—.

Up a long hill now, down into a valley—the road like a piece of white tape stretching ahead —past school houses, barns, market gardens; into dense woods, out on to level plains bare of a tree—one mad, devilish, brutal rush, with every man's eyes glued to the turn of the road ahead, which every half minute swerved, straightened, swerved again; now blocked by trees, now opening out, only to close, twist, and squirm anew. Great fun this, gambling with death, knowing that from behind any bush, beyond every hill crest, and around each curve there may spring something that will make assorted junk of your machine and send you to Ballyhack!

"Only one more hill," breathed the Sculptor, wiping the caked dust from his lips. Woo-oo-wow-o-o (nurse with a baby-carriage this time, running into the bushes like a frightened rabbit). "See the mill stream—that's it flashing in the sunlight! See the roof of the mill? That's Aston Knight's! Down brakes! All out—fifty-six miles in one hour and twenty-two minutes! Not bad!"

I sprang out—so did the Man from the Quarter—the flash from the mill stream glistening in the sunlight had set his blood to tingling; as for myself, no sheltering doorway had ever looked so inviting.

"Marie! *Marie!* Where's monsieur?" cried out the Sculptor from his seat beside the demon.

"Up-stairs, I think," answered a stout, gray-haired, rosy-cheeked woman, wiping her hand and arms on her apron as she spoke. She had started on a run from the brook's edge behind the house, where she had been washing, when she heard the shriek of the siren, but the machine had pulled up before she could reach the door-step.

"He went out early, but I think he's back now. Come in, come in, all of you. I'm glad to see you—so will he be."

Marie was cook, housemaid, valet, mother, doctor, and any number of things beside to Knight; just as in the village across the stream where she lived—or rather slept o' nights—she was bill-poster, bell-ringer, and town crier, to say nothing of her being the mother of eleven children, all her own—Knight being the adopted twelfth.

"The mill might as well be without water as without Marie," said the Sculptor. "Wait until you taste her baked trout—the chef at the Voisin is a fool beside her." We had all shaken the dear woman's hand now and had preceded her into the square hall filled with easels, fresh canvases, paintings hung on hooks to dry, pots of brushes, rain coats, sample racks of hats, and the like.

All this time the beast outside was snorting like a race-horse catching its breath after a run, the demon walking in front of it, examining its teeth, or mouth, or eyes, or whatever you do examine when you go poking around in front of it.

Up the narrow stairs, now in single file, and into a bedroom—evidently Knight's—full of canvases, sketching garb, fishing-rods and creels lining the walls; and then into another—evidently the guest's room—all lace covers, cretonne, carved chests, Louis XVI furniture, rare old portraits, and easy-chairs, the Sculptor opening each closet in turn, grumbling, "Just like him to try and fool us," but no trace of Knight.

Then the Sculptor threw up a window and thrust out his head, thus bringing clearer into view a stretch of meadow bordered with clumps of willows shading the rushing stream below.

"Louis! *Louis!* Where the devil are you, you brute of a painter?"

There came an halloo—faint—downstream.

"The beggar's at work somewhere in those bushes, and you couldn't get him out with dynamite until the light changed. Come along!"

There's no telling what an outdoor painter will submit to when an uncontrollable enthusiasm sweeps him off his feet, so to speak. I myself barely held my own (and within the year, too) on the top step of a crowded bridge in Venice in the midst of a cheering mob at a regatta, where I used the back of my gondolier for an easel, and again, when years ago, I clung to the platform of an elevated station in an effort to get, between the legs and bodies of the hurrying mob, the outlines of the spider-web connecting the two cities. I have watched, too, other painters in equally uncomfortable positions (that is, out-of-door painters; not steam-heated, easy-chair fellows, with pencil memoranda or photos to copy from) but it was the first time in all my varied experiences that I had ever come upon a painter standing up to his arm-pits in a swift-flowing mill or any other kind of stream, the water breaking against his body as a rock breasts a torrent, and he working away like mad on a 3 x 4 lashed to a huge ladder high enough to scale the mill's roof.

"Any fish?" yelled the Man from the Quarter.

"Yes, one squirming around my knees now — shipped him a minute ago — foot slipped. Awful glad to see you — stay where you are till I get this high light."

"Stay where I am!" bellowed the Sculptor. "Do you think I'm St. Peter or some long-legged crane that — "

"All right — I'm coming."

He had grabbed both sides of the ladder by this time, and with head in the crotch was sloshing ashore, the water squirting from the tops of his boots.

"Shake!" Mighty good of you fellows to come all the way down to see me. Here, you stone-cutter — help me off with these boots. Marie's getting luncheon. Don't touch that canvas — all this morning's work — got to work early." (It looked to be a finished picture to me.)

"STAY WHERE YOU ARE TILL I GET THIS HIGH LIGHT."

He was flat on the grass now, his legs in the air like an acrobat about to balance a globe, the water pouring from his wading boots, soaking the rest of him, all three of us tugging away — I at his head, the Sculptor at his feet. How Marie ever helped him squirm out of this diving-suit was more than I could tell.

We had started for the mill now, the Man from the Quarter lugging the boots, still hoping there might be some truth in the trout story, the Sculptor with the palette (big as a tea-tray), Knight with the ladder, and I with the wet canvas.

Again the cry rang out: "Marie! *Marie!*" and again the old woman started on a run — for the kitchen this time (she had been listening for this halloo — he generally came in wringing wet) — reappearing as we reached the hall door, her apron full of clothes swept from a drying line stretched before the big, all-embracing fire-place. These she carried ahead of us upstairs and deposited on the small iron bedstead in the painter's own room, Knight close behind, his wet socks making Man-Friday footprints in the middle of each well-scrubbed step. Once there, Knight dodged into a closet, wriggled himself loose, and was out again with half of Marie's apronful covering his chest and legs.

143

It was easy to see where the power of his brush lay. No timid, uncertain, niggling stroke ever came from that torso or forearm or thigh. He hewed with a broad axe, not with a chisel, and he hewed true — that was the joy of it. The men of Meissonier's time, like the old Dutchmen, worked from their knuckle joints. These new painters, in their new technique — new to some — old really, as that of Velasquez and Frans Hals — swing their brushes from their spinal columns down their forearms (Knight's biceps measure seventeen inches) and out through their finger-tips, with something of the rhythm and force of an old-time blacksmith welding a tire. Broad chests, big boilers, strong arms, straight legs, and stiff backbones have much to do with success in life — more than we give them credit for. Instead of measuring men's heads, it would be just as well, once in a while, to slip the tape around their chests and waists. Steam is what makes the wheels go round, and steam is well-digested fuel and a place to put it. With this equipment a man can put "GO" into his business, strength into his literature, virility into his brush; without it he may succeed in selling spool cotton or bobbins, may write pink poems for the multitude and cover wooden panels with cardinals and ladies of high degree

in real satin and life-like lace, but no part of his
output will take a full man's breath away.

Sunshine, flowers, open windows letting in
the cool breezes from meadow and stream ; an
old beamed ceiling, smoke-browned by countless
pipes; walls covered with sketches of every
nook and corner about us; a table for four,
heaped with melons, grapes, cheese, and flanked
by ten-pin bottles just out of the brook ; good-
fellowship, harmony of ideas, courage of convic-
tions — with no heads swelled to an unnatural
size; four appetites — enormous, prodigious appetites ; Knight for host and Marie as high cham-
berlainess, make the feast of Lucullus and the
afternoon teas of Cleopatra but so many quick
lunches served in the rush hour of a downtown
restaurant ! Not only were the trout-baked-in
cream (Marie's specialty) all that the Sculptor
had claimed for them, but the fried chicken,
soufflés — everything, in fact, that the dear
woman served — would have gained a Blue
Ribbon had she filled the plate of any committee-
man making the award.

With the coffee and cigars (cigarettes had
been smoked with every course — it was that
kind of a feast) the four mouths had a breathing
spell.

Up to this time the talk had been a staccato performance between mouthfuls :

" Yes — came near smashing a donkey — don't care if I do — no — no gravy " (Sculptor). "Let me put an extra bubble in your glass " (Knight). "These fish are as firm as the Adirondack trout" (Man from the Quarter). " More cream — thank you. Marie ! " (Knight, of course) " more butter." "Donkey wasn't the only thing we missed — grazed a baby carriage and —" (Scribe). " I'm going to try a red ibis after luncheon and a miller for a tail fly — pass the melon " (Man from the Quarter): That sort of hurried talk without logical beginning or ending.

But now each man had a comfortable chair, and filled it with shoulders hidden deep in its capacious depths, and legs straight out, only the arms and hands free enough to be within reach of the match-safe and thimble glasses. And with the ease and comfort of it all the talk itself slowed down to a pace more in harmony with that peace which passeth all understanding — unless you've a seat at the table.

The several masters of the outdoor school were now called up, their merits discussed and their failings hammered : Thaulow, Sorolla y Bastida, the new Spanish wonder, whose exhibition the month before had astonished and delighted

146

Paris: the Glasgow school; Zorn, Sargent, Winslow Homer—all the men of the direct, forceful school, men who swing their brushes from their spines instead of their finger-tips — were slashed into and made mincemeat of or extolled to the skies. Then the "patty-pats," with their little dabs of yellow, blue, and red, in imitation of the master Monet; the "slick and slimies," and the "woollies" — the men who essayed the vague, mysterious, and obscure — were set up and knocked down one after the other, as is the custom with all groups of painters the world over when the never-ending question of technique is tossed into the middle of the arena.

Outdoor work next came into review and the discomforts and hardships a painter must go through to get what he is after, the Man from the Quarter defending the sit-by-the-fire fellows.

"No use making a submarine diver of yourself, Knight," he growled. "Go and look at it and then come home and paint the impression and put something of yourself into it."

Knight threw his head back and laughed. "I'd rather put the brook in — all of it."

"But I don't see why you've got to get soaked to the skin every time you want to make a sketch."

147

"The soaking is what helps," replied Knight, reaching for a match. "I like to feel I'm drinksome of it in. Then, when you're right in the middle of it you don't put on any airs and try to improve on what's before you and spoil it with detail. One dimple on a girl's cheek is charming; two — and you send for the doctor. And she's so simple when you look into her face — I'm talking of the brook now, not the girl — and it's so easy to put her down as she is, not the form and color only, but the *mood* in which you find her. A brook is worse, really, than your best girl in the lightning changes she can go through — laughing, crying, coquetting — just as the mood seizes her. There, for instance, hanging over your head is a 'gray day'" — and he pointed to one of his running-water sketches tacked to the wall. "I tried to cheer her up a little with touches of warm tones here and there — all lies — same kind you tell your own chickabiddy when she's blue — but she wouldn't have it and cried straight ahead for four hours until the sun came out; but I was through by that time and waded ashore. You can see for yourselves how unhappy she was." He spoke as if the sketch was alive — and it was.

"But I always work out of doors that way,"

148

he continued. "In winter up in Holland I sit in furs and wooden shoes, and often have to put alcohol in my water-cups to keep my colors from freezing. My big picture of 'The Torrent' —the one in the Toledo Art Gallery—was painted in January, and out of doors. As for the brushwork, I try to do the best I can. I used to tickle up things I painted; some of the fellows at Julian's believed in that, and so did Fleury and Lefebvre to some extent."

"And when did you get over it?" I asked.

"When my father persuaded me to send a bold sketch to the Volney Club, which I had done to please myself, and which they hung and bought. So I said to myself: 'Why trim, clean up, and make pretty a picture, when by simply painting what I love in nature in a free, breezy manner while my enthusiasm lasts—and it generally lasts until I get through;—sometimes it spills over to the next day—I please myself and a lot of people beside."

We were all on our feet now examining the sketches—all running-brook studies—most of them made in that same pair of high-water boots. No one but the late Fritz Thaulow approaches him in giving the reality of this most difficult subject for an outdoor painter. The ocean surf repeats itself in its recurl and swash and by close watching a painter has often a chance to use his "second barrel," so to speak, but the upturned face of an unruly brook is not only million-tinted and endless in its expression, but so sensitive in its reflections that every passing cloud and patch of blue above it saddens or cheers it.

"Yes, painting water is enough to drive you mad," burst out Knight, "but I don't intend to paint anything else — not for years, any way. Hired the mill so I could paint the water running *away* from you downhill. That's going to take a good many years to get hold of, but I'm going to stick it out. I can't always paint it from the banks, not if I want to study the middle ripples at my feet, and these are the ones that run out of your canvas just above your name-plate. *Got* to stand in it, I tell you. Then you get the drawing, and the drawing is what counts. Oh, I love it!" Knight stretched his big arms and legs and sprang from his chair.

"Really, fellows, I don't know anything about it. All I do is to let myself go. I always *feel* more than I *see,* and so my brush has a devil of a job to keep up. Marie! *Marie!*"

Had the good woman been a mile down the brook she could have heard him — she was only in the next room. "Bring in the boots — two

150

pairs this time — we're going fishing. And,
Marie — has the chauffeur had anything to eat?"

"Yes, monsieur."

"Anything to drink?"

"No, monsieur."

"*What!* Hand him this," and he grabbed
a half-empty bottle from the table.

I sprang forward and caught it before Marie
got her fingers around it.

"Not if I know it!" I cried. "We've got
to get back to Dives. When he lands me inside my garden at the inn he shall have a magnum, but not a drop till he does."

When the two had gone the Sculptor and I
leaned back in our chairs and lighted fresh cigars.
My enthusiasm has not cooled for the sports of
my youth. With a comfortable stool, a well-
filled basket, and a long jointed rod, I, like many
another staid old painter, can still get an amaz-
ing amount of enjoyment watching a floating
cork, but I didn't propose to follow those two
lunatics. I knew the Man from the Quarter—
had known him from the day of his birth —
and knew what he would do and where he
would go (over his head sometimes) for a poor
devil of a fish half as long as his finger, and I
had had positive evidence of what the other web-

footed duck thought of ice-cold water. No, I'd take a little sugar in mine, if you please, and put a drop of — but the Sculptor had already foreseen and was then forestalling my needs, so we leaned back in our chairs once more.

Again the talk covered wide reaches.

"Great boy, Knight," broke out the Sculptor in a sudden burst of enthusiasm over his friend. "You ought to see him handle a crowd when he's at work. He knows the French people—never gets mad. He bought a calf for Marie last week, and drove it home himself. Told me it had ten legs, four heads, and twenty tails before he got it here. Old woman lost hers and Knight bought her another — he'd bring her a herd if she wanted it. All the way from the market the boys kept up a running fire of criticism. When the ringleader came too near, Knight sprang at him with a yelp like a dog's. The boy was so taken aback that he ran. Then Knight roared with laughter, and in an instant the whole crowd were his friends — two of them helped him get the calf out of town. When a French crowd laughs with you you can do anything with them. He had had more fun bringing home that calf, he told me, than he'd had for weeks, and he's a wonder at having a good time."

Then followed — much of which was news to

me — an account of the painter's earlier life and successes.

He was born in Paris, August 3, 1873; his father, Ridgway Knight, the distinguished painter, and his mother, who was Rebecca Morris Webster, both being Philadelphians. Not only is he, therefore, of true American descent, but his eight great-grandparents were Americans, dating back to Thomas Ridgway, who was born in Delaware in 1713. Thus by both the French and American laws he is an American citizen.

At fourteen he was sent to Chigwell School in England by his father, to have "art knocked out of him" by the uncongenial surroundings of the quiet old school where the great William Penn had been taught to read and write. He left in 1890, having won the Special Classical Prize, Oxford and Cambridge certificate Prize, besides prizes for carpentering, gymnasium, running, and "putting the weight."

At home the boy always drew and painted for pleasure, as well as at school during the half-holidays. Some water-colors made during a holiday trip in Brittany in 1890 decided his father to allow him to follow art as a career. He entered Julian's studio, with Jules Lefebvre and Tony Robert-Fleury as professors in 1891, and studied from the nude during the five following winters. His principal work was, however, done in the country at and around Poissy, under the guidance of his father.

His exhibits in the Paris Salon (*artistes Français*) were twenty-four oils and water-colors from 1894 to 1906, obtaining an honorable mention in 1901 with the " Thames at Whitchurch"; a gold medal, third class, in 1905, with "The Torrent"; and a gold medal, second class, in 1906, with his triptych "The Giant Cities" (New York, Paris, London), which makes him *hors concours*, with the great distinction of being the first American landscape painter to get two Salon gold medals in two consecutive years. He won also a bronze medal in the American section of the Paris Universal Exhibition in 1900 with a water-color, and a gold medal of honor at Rheims, Cherbourg, Geneva, and Nantes.

His most important pictures are: "The Torrent," 4½ x 6 feet, owned by the Toledo Art Gallery; "The Abandoned Mill," 4½ x 6 feet; "The End of the Island," 6 x 8 feet; "Clisson Castle," 3 x 4½ feet, a water-color; "After the Storm," 3 x 5 feet; and "Winter in Holland," 3 x 4 feet.

I had listened to the Sculptor's brief account of his friend's progress with calm attention, but it had not altered my opinion of the man or his genius. None of it really interested me except that somebody beside myself had found out the lad's qualities — for to me he is still a lad. None of the jury who made the awards ever looked below the paint — that is, if they were like other juries the world over. They saw the brush-mark, no doubt, but they missed the breeze that came with it — was its life, really — a breeze that swept through and out of him, blowing side by side with genius and good health — a wind of destiny, perhaps, that will carry him to climes that other men know not of.

But what a refreshing thing, this breeze, to come out of a man, and what a refreshing kind of a man for it to come out of! No pose, no effort to fill a No. 8 hat with a No. 7 head; just a simple, conscientious, hard-working young painter, humble-minded in the presence of his goddess, and full to overflowing with an uncontrollable spontaneity. This in itself was worth risking one's neck to see.

Again the cry rang out, "Marie!" and two half-drowned water-rats stepped in; the Man from the Quarter in his underpinning — his pair of boots leaked and he had stripped them off — and Knight with his own half full of water. Both roared with laughter at Marie tugging at

155

the huge white-rubber boots, the floor she had scrubbed so conscientiously spattered with sand and water.

Then began the customary recriminations: "Hadn't been for you I wouldn't have lost him!" "What had I to do with it?" etc., etc.—the same old story when neither gets a bite.

That night, bumping over the thank-you-marms, flashing through darkened villages, and scooting in a dead heat along ribboned roads ghostly white in the starlight, on the way back to my garden—and we did arrive safely, and the chauffeur had his magnum (that is, his share of it)—I could not help saying to myself:

"Yes, it's good to be young and bouyant, but it's better to be one's self."

FIDDLES

THIS is Marny's story, not mine. He had a hammer in his hand at the time and a tack between his teeth.

"Going to hang Fiddles right under the old fellow's head," he burst out. "That's where he belongs. I'd have given a ten-acre if he could have drawn a bead on that elk himself. Fiddles behind a .44 Winchester and that old buck browsing to windward"—and he nodded at the elk's head—"would have made the village Mayor sit up and think. What a picturesque liar you are, Fiddles"— here the point of the tack was pressed into the plaster with Marny's fat thumb —"and what a good-for-nothing, breezy, lovable vagabond"—(Bang! Bang! Hammer at play now)—"you could be when you tried. There!"

Marny stepped back and took in the stuffed head and wide-branched antlers of the magnificent elk (five feet six from skull to tips) and the small, partly faded miniature of a young man in a student cap and high-collared coat.

I waited and let him run on. It is never wise

to interrupt Marny. He will lose the thread of his talk if you do, and though he starts off immediately on another lead, and one, perhaps equally graphic, he has left you suspended in mid-air so far as the tale you were getting interested in is concerned. Who Fiddles was and why his Honor the Mayor should sit up and think; why, too, the miniature of the young man—and he *was* young and remarkably good-looking, as I well knew, having seen the picture many times before on his mantel—should now be suspended below the elk's head, would come out in time if I loosened my ear-flaps and buttoned up my tongue, but not if I reversed the operation.

"Ah, you young fraud," he went on—the position of both head and miniature pleased him now—"do you remember the time I hauled you out from under the table when the hucksters were making a door-mat of your back; and the time I washed you off at the pump, and what you said to the gendarme, and— No, you never remembered anything. You'd rather sprawl out on the grass, or make eyes at Gretchen or the landlady—fifty, if she was a day—maybe fifty-five, and yet she fell in love" (this last was addressed directly to me; it had been reminiscent before that, fired at the ceiling, at the hangings

158

in his sumptuous studio, or the fire crackling on the hearth), "fell in love with that tramp—a boy of twenty-two, mind you— Ah! but what a rounder he was! Such a trim, well-knit figure; so light and nimble on his feet; such a pair of eyes in his head, leaking tears one minute and flashing hate the next. And his mouth! I tried, but I couldn't paint it—nobody could—so I did his profile; one of those curving, seductive mouths you sometimes see on a man, that quivers when he smiles, the teeth gleaming between the moist lips."

I had lassoed a chair with my foot by this time, had dragged it nearer the fire, and had settled myself in another.

"Funny name, though for a German," I remarked carelessly — quite as if the fellow's patronymic had already formed part of the discussion.

"Had to call him something for short," Marny retorted. "Feudels-Shimmer was what they called him in Rosengarten — Wilhelm Feudels-Shimmer. I tried all of it at first, then I bit off the Shimmer, and then the Wilhelm, and ran him along on Feudels for a while, then it got down to Fuddles, and at last to Fiddles, and there it stuck. Just fitted him, too. All he wanted was a bow, and I furnished that—

enough of the devil's resin to set him going —
and out would roll jigs, lullabys, fandangoes,
serenades — anything you wanted: anything to
which his mood tempted him."

Marny had settled into his chair now, and
had stretched his fat legs toward the blaze, his
middle distance completely filling the space between the arms. He had pushed himself over
many a ledge with this same pair of legs and on
this same rotundity, his hand on his Winchester,
before his first ball crashed through the shoulder
of the big elk whose glass eyes were now looking down upon Fiddles and ourselves — and he
would do it again on another big-horn when the
season opened. You wouldn't have thought so
had you dropped in upon us and scanned his
waist measure, but then, of course, you don't
know Marny.

Again Marny's eyes rested for a moment on
the miniature; then he went on:

"We were about broke when I painted it,"
he said. "There was a fair of some sort in the
village, and I got an old frame for half a mark
in a pawnshop, borrowed a coat from Fritz, the
stableman, squeezed Fiddles into it, stuck a student's cap on his head, made it look a hundred
years old — the frame was all of that — and tried
to sell it as a portrait of a ' Gentleman of the

Last Century,' but it wouldn't work. Fiddles's laugh gave it away. 'Looks like you,' the old man said. 'Yes, it's my brother,' he blurted out, slapping the dealer on the back."

"Where did you pick Fiddles up?" I asked.

"Nowhere," answered Marny; "he picked me up. That is, the gendarme did who had him by the coat collar."

"'This fellow insists you know him,' said the officer of the law. 'He says that he is honest and that this rabbit'—here he pointed to a pair of long ears sticking out of a game bag—'is one he shot with the Mayor this morning. Is this true?'

"Now if there is one thing, old man," continued Marny, "that gets me hot around the collar, it is to see a brother sportsman arrested for killing anything that can fly, run, or swim. So I rose from my sketching stool and looked him over: his eyes—not a bit of harm in 'em; his loose necktie thrown over one shoulder; trim waist, and so on down to the leather leggings buttoned to his knees. If he was a poacher and subject to the law, he certainly was the most picturesque specimen I had met in many a day. I had, of course, never laid eyes on him before, having been but a few days in the village, but that made the situation all the more

161

interesting. To rescue a friend would be commonplace, to rescue a stranger smacked of adventure.

"I uncovered my head and bowed to the ground. 'His Honor shoots almost every day, your Excellency,' I said to the gendarme. 'I have seen him frequently with his friends—this young man is no doubt one of them—Let—me—think—was it this morning, or yesterday, I met the Mayor? It is at best a very small rabbit'—here I fingered the head and ears—'and would probably have died of hunger anyway. However, if any claim should be made by the farmer I will pay the damages'—this with a lordly air, and I with only a week's board in my pocket.

"The gendarme released his hold and stood looking at the young fellow. The day was hot and the village lock-up two miles away. That the rabbit was small and the Mayor an inveterate sportsman were also undeniable facts.

"'Next time,' he said sententiously, with a scowl, 'do you let his Honor carry the game home in his own bag,' and he walked away.

"Oh, you just ought to have seen Fiddles skip around when a turn in the road shut out the cocked hat and cross-belts, and heard him pour out his thanks. 'His name was Wilhelm,' he cried out; it had only been by chance that he had got separated from his friends. Where did I live? Would I let him give me the rabbit for a stew for my dinner? Was I the painter who had come to the inn? If so he had heard of me. Could he and his friends call upon me that night? He would never forget my kindness. What was the use of being a gentleman if you couldn't help another gentleman out of a scrape? As for Herr Rabbit—the poor little Herr Rabbit— here he stroked his fur—what more honorable end than gracing the table of the Honorable Painter? Ah, these dogs of the law—when would they learn not to meddle with things that did not concern them?"

"And did Fiddles come to your inn, Marny?" I asked, merely as a prod to keep him going.

"Yes, a week later, and with the same gendarme. The cobbler in the village, who sat all day long pegging at his shoes, and who, it seemed, was watch-goose for the whole village and knew the movements of every inhabitant, man, woman, and child, and who for some reason hated Fiddles, on being interviewed by the gendarme, had stated positively that the Mayor had *not* passed his corner with his gun and four dogs on the day of Fiddles's arrest. This being the case, the gendarme had rearrested the culprit, and would have taken him at once to the lock-up had not Fiddles threatened the officer with false arrest. Would the Herr Painter accompany the officer and himself to the house of the Mayor and settle the matter as to whether his Honor was or was not out hunting on that particular morning?

"All this time Fiddles was looking about the dining-room of the inn, taking in the supper-table, the rows of mugs, especially the landlady, who was frightened half out of her wits by Cocked Hat's presence, and more especially still little Gretchen — such a plump, rosy-cheeked, blue-eyed little Dutch girl — with two Marguerite pig-tails down her back. (Gretchen served the beer, and was the life of the place. 'Poor young man!' she said to the landlady, who had by this time come to the same conclusion—'and he is so good-looking and with such lovely eyes.')

"When we got to the Mayor's the old fellow was asleep in a big armchair, his pipe out, his legs far apart—a keg-shaped kind of a man, with a head flattened on his shoulders like a stove-lid, who said 'Ach Gott' every five minutes, and spluttered when he talked.

"I went in first, leaving the two on the porch until I should send for them. I didn't know how things were going to turn out and had become a little anxious. I had run up from Munich for

164

a few weeks' outdoor work and wanted to stay out, not behind iron bars for abetting crime.

"'Your Supreme Highness,' I began, 'I have heard of your great prowess as a sportsman, and so I wanted to pay my respects. I, too, am a shootist—an American shootist.' Here I launched out on our big game (I had been six months in the Rockies before I came abroad, and knew what I was talking about). He was wide awake by this time and was listening. Dropping into the chair which he had drawn up for me, I told him of our elk—'As big as horses, your Honor'; of our mountain lions—savage beasts that could climb trees and fall upon the defenseless; of our catamounts, deer, wolves, bears, foxes—all these we killed without molestation from anybody; I told him how all American sportsmen were like the Nimrods of old. How galling, then, for a true shootist to be misunderstood, decried, denounced, and arrested for so insignificant a beastie as a rabbit! This indignity my very dear friend, Herr Wilhelm Fuedels-Shimmer, had suffered—a most estimable young man—careless, perhaps, in his interpretation of the law, but who would not be—that is, what sportsman would not be? I had in Wilhelm's defense not only backed up his story, but I had gone so far as to hazard the opinion to the officer of that law, that it was not on some uncertain Tuesday or Friday or Saturday, but on that very Wednesday, that his Supreme Highness had been wont to follow with his four accomplished dogs the tracks of the nimble cotton-tail. Would his Highness, therefore, be good enough to concentrate his giant brain on his past life and fish from out his memory the exact day on which he last hunted? While that was going on I would excuse myself long enough to bring in the alleged criminal.

"Fiddles stepped in with the easy grace of a courtier accustomed to meeting a Mayor every day of his life, and, after a confirmatory wink from me, boldly asserted that he had followed behind his Honor—had really assisted in driving the game his way. His Honor might not remember his face, but he surely must remember that his Honorable Honor had extraordinarily good luck that day. The rabbit in controversy—a very small, quite a baby rabbit—was really one his Honorable and Most Supreme Highness had himself wounded, and which he, Fiddles, had finished. He was bringing it to his Honor when the estimable gendarme had stopped him.

"'And what day was that?' interrupted the Mayor.

"'On last Wednesday.'

" 'The cobbler said it was Tuesday,' insisted Cocked Hat. 'On this point hangs the case. Now on which day did your Honor take the field with your dogs ? '

"There was a dead silence, during which the Mayor's eyes rested on the culprit. Fiddles returned the look, head up, a smile on his lips that would have fooled the devil himself. Then his Honor turned to me and said : ' My memory is not always very good, but this time the cobbler's — who is a meddlesome person — is even more defective. Yes, I think it quite possible I was hunting on last Wednesday. I can sympathize with the young man as to the size of the rabbit. They are running very small this year. My decision, therefore, is that you can let the young man go.'

"Oh, but that was a great night at the inn. Gretchen was so happy that she spilled the beer down the apothecary's back and the landlady could talk of nothing but Fiddles's release. But the real fun began an hour later, when shouts for the Herr Mähler, interwoven with the music of a concertina, made me step to the door. Outside, in the road, stood four young men — all pals of Fiddles, all bareheaded, and all carrying lanterns. They had come to crown the American with a gold chaplet cut from gilt paper, after which I was to be conducted to the public house where bumpers of beer were to be drunk until the last pfennig was spent.

"On hearing this, Gretchen, the landlady, the apothecary, the hostler, and the stable-boy— not the cobbler, you may be sure — burst forth with cries of : ' Hip ! Hip ! — Hock ! Donder und Blitzen ! ' or whatever they do yell when they are mad with joy.

" Then the landlady broke out in a fresh place : ' No public-house for you ! This is my treat ! All of you come inside. Gretchen, get the mugs full — all the mugs — Sit down ! Sit down ! The Herr Painter at the top of the table, the Herr Feudels-Shimmer on the right; all the other Herrs anywhere in between. Hock the Mähler ! Hock the Hunter ! Hock everybody but the cobbler ! ' Here a groan went round. ' Hock ! Hip and Blather skitzen for the good and honorable Mayor, who always loves the people ! '

" ' And Hock ! too, for the honorable and good gendarme ! ' laughed Fiddles, dropping into his chair. ' But for him I would be in the lock-up instead of basking in the smiles of two such lovely women as the fascinating landlady and the bewitching Gretchen.'

" After that Fiddles and I became inseparable. That I hadn't a mark over my expenses to give

him in return for his services — and there was
nothing he would not do for me — made no difference. He wouldn't take any wages; all he
wanted was to carry my traps, to sit by me while
I worked; wake me up in the morning, be the
last to wish me good night. Soon it became a
settled fact that, while the landlady fed two
mouths — mine and Fiddles's — and provided
two beds — Fiddles in the garret — my single
board bill covered all the items. 'That is the
Herr Painter and his servant,' she would say to
inquiring strangers who watched us depart for a
day's work, Fiddles carrying my easel and
traps.

"This went on for weeks — might have gone
on all summer but for the events which followed
a day's outing. We had spent the morning
sketching, and on our way home had stood opposite a wide-open gate — a great baronial affair
with a coat of arms in twisted iron, the whole
flanked by two royal lamps.

"'Step inside, Master,' said Fiddles. 'It is
hot, and there is a seat under that tree; there
we will get cool.'

"'It's against the rules, Fiddles, and I don't
know these people.'

"'Then I'll introduce you.'

"He was half-way across the grass by this

time and within reach of a wooden bench, when
an old lady stepped out from behind a tree — a
real old aristocrat in black silk and white ruffles.
She had a book in her hand, and had evidently
been reading.

"You should have seen the bow Fiddles gave
her, and the courtesy she returned.

"'Madame the Baroness,' said the rascal,
with an irradiating smile as I approached them,
'has been good enough to ask us to accompany
her to the house. Permit me, Madame, to
present my friend, a distinguished American
painter who is visiting our country, and who
was so entranced at the beauty of your grounds
and the regal splendor of your gate and château
that rather than disappoint him—'

"'You are both doubly welcome, gentlemen.
This way, please,' replied the old lady with a
dip of her aristocratic head; and before I knew
it we were seated in an oak-panelled dining-
room with two servants in livery tumbling over
each other in their efforts to find the particular
wine best suited to our palates.

"Fiddles sipped his Rudesheimer with the air
of a connoisseur, blinking at the ceiling now and
then after the manner of expert wine tasters,
and complimenting the old lady meanwhile on
the quality of the vintage. I confined myself to

a glass of sherry and a biscuit, while Fiddles, rising from his seat, later on, stood enraptured before this portrait and that, commenting on their coloring, ending by drawing an ancient book from the library and going into ecstasies over the binding and type.

"On our way home to the inn from the château there was, so far as I could see, no change in Fiddles's manner. Neither was his speech or gait at all affected by the bottle of Rudesheimer (and he managed to get away with it all). I mention this because it is vitally important to what follows. Only once did he seem at all excited, and that was when he passed the cobbler's corner. But then he was always excited when he passed the cobbler seated at work—so much so sometimes that I have seen him shake his fist at him. To-day he merely tightened his jaw, stopped for a moment as if determined to step in and have it out with him (the cobbler, I afterward found out, was to leave the village for good the next day, his trade having fallen off, owing to his being so unpopular), and then, as if changing his mind, followed along after me, muttering: 'Spy —informer—beast—' as I had often heard him do before.

"Judge of my astonishment then, when, an hour later, Gretchen came running into my room wringing her hands—I had caught him kissing her the night before—and burst out with:

"'He is under the table—the truckster's feet on him— He is there like a dog— Oh, it is dreadful! Mine Herr—won't you come!'

"'Who is under the table?'

"'Wilhelm.'

"'Where?'

"'At the public-house.'

"'How do you know?'

"'Fritz, the stable-boy has just seen him.'

"'What's the matter with him?'

"Gretchen hung her head, and the tears streamed down her cheeks.

"'He is—he is— Oh, Meinherr—it is not the beer—nobody ever gets that way with our beer—it is something he—'

"'Drunk!'

"'Yes, dead drunk, and under the table like a hog in the mud— Oh, my poor Wilhelm! Oh, who has been so wicked to you! Oh! Oh!' and she ran from the room.

"I started on the run, Gretchen and the good landlady close behind. If the Rudesheimer had upset Fiddles it had worked very slowly; maybe it had revived an old conquered thirst, and the cheap cognac at the public-house was the result. That he was not a man of humble birth, nor one

without home refinements, I had long since di-
vined. Had I not suspected it before, his manner in presenting me to the old Baroness, and
his behavior in the dining-hall, especially toward
the servants, would have opened my eyes.
How then could such a man in an hour become
so besotted a brute?

"And yet every word of Gretchen's story was
true. Not only was Fiddles drunk, soggy, help-
lessly drunk, but from all accounts he was in that
same condition when he had staggered into the
place, and, falling over a table, had rolled himself against the wall. There he had lain, out of
the way, except when some dram-drinking
driver's heavy cowhide boots had made a door-
mat of his yielding body — not an unusual oc-
currence, by the way, at the roadside taverns
frequented by the lower classes.

We worked over him, calling him by name,
propping him up against the wall, only to have
him sag back; and finally, at the suggestion of one
of the truckmen — he was in a half-comatose state
really from the liquor he had absorbed — we carried him out into the stable yard, and I held his
shapely head, with its beautiful hair a-frowze,
while a stream of cold water from the pump
struck the back of his head and neck.

"The poor fellow stared around wildly as the

173

chill reached his nerves and tried to put his arm around me, then he toppled over again and lay like a log. Nothing was left but to pick him up bodily and carry him home; that I did with Fritz's, the stable-boy's, help, Gretchen carrying his cap, and the landlady following behind with his coat, which I had stripped off when his head went under the pump. The bystanders didn't care — one drunken man more or less made no difference — but both of the women were in tears. 'Poor Wilhelm! Somebody had drugged him; some wicked men had played a trick,' etc., etc. I thought of the Rudesheimer, and then dismissed it from my mind. Something stronger than Rhine wine had wrought this change.

"We laid him flat out on a cot in a room on the second floor, and dragged it near the open window so he could get the air from the garden, and left him, I taking the precaution to lock the door to prevent his staggering downstairs and breaking his neck.

"The next morning, before I was dressed, in fact, a row downstairs brought me into the hall outside my door, where I stood listening over the banister. Then came the tramp of men, and three gendarmes mounted the steps and halted at Fiddles's door.

"Bang! bang! went the hilt of a short-sword

on the panel. 'Open, in the name of the law.'

"'What for?' I demanded. Getting drunk was not a crime in Rosengarten, especially when the offender had been tucked away in bed.

"'For smashing the face of a citizen—a worthy cobbler—the night before, at the hour of eight, —just as he was closing his shutters. The cobbler lay insensible until he had been found by the patrol. He had, however, recognized Fuedels-Shimmer as the—'

"'But, gentleman, Herr Fiddles was dead drunk at eight o'clock; he hasn't stirred out of the room since. Here is the key,' and I unlocked the door and we all stepped in, Gretchen and the landlady close behind. They had told the officers the same story downstairs, but they would not believe it.

"At the intrusion, Fiddles rose to a sitting posture and stared wonderingly. He was sober enough now, but his heavy sleep still showed about his eyes.

"The production of the key, my positive statement, backed by the women, and Fiddles's wondering gaze, brought the gendarmes to a halt for a moment, but his previous arrest was against him, and so the boy was finally ordered to put on his clothes and accompany them to the lock-up.

"I got into the rest of my duds, and began waving the American flag and ordering out gunboats. I insisted that the cobbler had lied before in accusing Fiddles of shooting the rabbit, as was well known, and he would lie again. Fiddles was my friend, my servant — a youth of incorruptible character. It is true he had been intoxicated the night before, and that I had in consequence put him to bed, but that was entirely due to the effects of some very rare wine which he had drunk at a luncheon given in his honor and mine by our very dear friend the Baroness Morghenslitz, who had entertained us at her princely home. This, with the heat of the day, had been, etc., etc,

"The mention of the distinguished woman's name caused another halt. Further consultation ensued, resulting in the decision that we all adjourn to the office of the Mayor. If, after hearing our alibi — one beyond dispute, and submitting our evidence (Exhibit A, the key, which they must admit exactly fitted the lock of Fiddles's bedroom door), his Honor could still be made to believe the perjured testimony of the cobbler — Fiddles's enemy, as had been abundantly proved in the previous rabbit case, when the same mendacious half-soler and heeler had informed on my friend — well and good; but if

176

not, then, the resources of my Government would be set in motion for the young man's release.

"The Mayor's first words were: 'Ah, you have come again, is it, Meinherr Marny; and it is the same young man, too, Herr Fuddles. Well, well, it is much trouble that you have.' (I'd give it to you in German, old man, but you wouldn't understand it—this to me in a sort of an aside.)

"Fiddles never moved a muscle of his face. You would have thought that he was the least interested man in the room. Only once did his features relax, and that was when the cobbler arrived with his head swathed in bandages. Then a grim smile flickered about the corners of his mouth, as if fate had at last overtaken his enemy.

"Of course, the Mayor dismissed the case. Gretchen's tearful, pleading face, the landlady's positive statement of helping put the dear young gentleman to bed; the key and the use I had made of it; the reluctant testimony of the offi-cers, who had tried the knob and could not get in until I had turned the lock, together with the well-known animosity of the cobbler (and all because Fiddles had ridiculed his workmanship on a pair of shoes the boy had left with him to be half-soled), turned the tide in the lad's favor and sent us all back to the inn rejoicing.

"Some weeks later Fiddles came into my room, locked the door, pulled down the shades, looked under the bed, in the closet and behind the curtains, and sat down in front of me. (I had to return to Munich the next day, and this would be our last night together.)

"'You have been very good to me, Master,' he said with a choke in his voice. 'I love people who are good to me; I hate those who are not. I have been that way all my life—it would have been better for me if I hadn't.' Then he leaned forward and took my hand. 'I want you to do something more for me; I want you to promise me you'll take me home to America with you when you go. I'm tired dodging these people. I want to get somewhere where I can shoot and hunt and fish, and nobody can stop me. I snared that rabbit; been snaring them all summer; going to keep on snaring them after you're gone. I love to hunt them—love the fun of it—born that way. And I've got something else to tell you'—here a triumphant smile flashed over his face—'I smashed that cobbler!'

"'You, Fiddles!' I laughed. 'Why, you were dead drunk, and I put you under the pump and—'

178

" ' Yes, I know you thought so—I intended you should. I heard every word that you said, and what little Gretchen said—dear little Gretchen! I had studied it all out, and to play drunk seemed the best way to get at the brute, and it was; they'd have proved it on me if I hadn't fooled them that way—' and again his eyes snapped and his face flushed as the humor of the situation rose in his mind. ' You'll forgive me, won't you? Don't tell Gretchen.' The light in his eyes was gone now. I'd rather she'd think me drunk than vulgar, and it was vulgar, and maybe cowardly, to hit him, but I couldn't help that either, and I'm not sorry I did it.'

" ' But I locked you in,' I persisted. Was this some invention of his fertile imagination, or was it true?

" ' Yes, you locked the door,' he answered, as he broke into a subdued laugh. ' I dropped from the window sill when it got dark—it wasn't high, about fifteen feet, and the water-spout helped — ran down the back way, gave him a crack as he opened the door, and was back in bed by the help of the same spout before he had come to. He was leaving the next day and it was my only chance. I wasn't out of the room five minutes — maybe less. You'll forgive me that too, won't you?' "

Marny stopped and looked into the smouldering coals. For a brief instant he did not speak. Then he rose from his chair, crossed the room, took the miniature from the wall where he had hung it and looked at it steadily.

"What a delightful devil you were, Fiddles. And you were so human."

"Is he living yet?" I asked.

"No, he died in Gretchen's arms. I kept my promise, and two months later went back to the village to bring him to America with me, but a forester's bullet had ended him. It was on the Baroness's grounds, too. He wouldn't halt and the guard fired. Think of killing such an adorable savage—and all because the blood of the primeval man boiled in his veins. Oh, it was damnable!"

"And you know nothing more about him? Where he came from?" The story had strangely moved me. "Were there no letters or notebooks? Nothing to show who he really was?"

"Only an empty envelope postmarked 'Berlin.' This had reached him the day before, and was sealed with a coat of arms in violet wax."

HOMO

DINNER was over, and Mme. Constantin and her guests were seated under the lighted candles in her cosey salon.

With the serving of the coffee and cigarettes, pillows had been adjusted to bare shoulders, stools moved under slippered feet, and easy lounges pushed nearer the fire. Greenough, his long body aslant, his head on the edge of a chair, his feet on the hearth rug, was blowing rings to the ceiling. Bayard, the African explorer, and the young Russian Secretary, Ivan Petrovski, had each the end of a long sofa, with pretty Mme. Petrovski and old Baron Sleyde between them, while Mme. Constantin lay nestled like a kitten among the big and little cushions of a divan.

The dinner had been a merry one, with every brain at its best; this restful silence was but another luxury. Only the Baron rattled on. A duel of unusual ferocity had startled Paris, and the old fellow knew its every detail. Mme. Petrovski was listening in a languid way.

"Dead, isn't he?" she asked in an indifferent tone, as being the better way to change the subject. Duels did not interest the young bride.

"No," answered the Baron, flicking the ashes from his cigarette—"going to get well, so Mercier, who operated, told a friend of mine to-day."

"Where did they fight?" she asked, as she took a fresh cigarette from her case. "Ivan told me, but I forgot."

"At Surenne, above the bridge. You know the row of trees by the water; we walked there the day we dined at the Cycle."

"Both of them fools!" cried the Russian from the depths of his seat. "La Clou wasn't worth it—she's getting fat."

Greenough drew his long legs back from the fender and, looking toward the young Secretary, said in a decided tone:—

"I don't agree with you, Ivan. Served the beggar right; the only pity is that he's going to get well."

"But she wasn't his wife," remarked Mme. Petrovski with increased interest, as she lighted her cigarette.

"No matter, he loved her," returned the Englishman, straightening in his seat and squaring his broad shoulders.

182

"And so did the poor devil whom Mercier sewed up," laughed the old Baron, his eyes twinkling.

Mme. Constantin raised her blonde head from the edge of the divan.

"Is there any wrong, you dear Greenough, you would forgive where a woman is concerned?"

"Plenty. Any wrong that you would commit, my dear lady, for instance; but not the kind the Baron refers to."

"But why do you Englishmen always insist on an eye for an eye and a tooth for a tooth? Can't you make some allowance for the weakness of human nature?" she asked, smiling.

"But why only Englishmen?" demanded Greenough. "All nationalities feel alike where a man's honor and the honor of his home are concerned. It is only the punishment that differs. The Turk, for instance, bowstrings you or tries to, for peeping under his wife's veil; the American shoots you at sight for speaking slightingly of his daughter. Both are right in a way. I am not brutal; I am only just, and I tell you there is only one way of treating a man who has robbed you dishonestly of the woman you love, and that is to finish him so completely that the first man called in

183

will be the undertaker—not the surgeon. I am not talking at random—I know a case in point, which always sets me blazing when I think of it. He was at the time attached to our embassy at Berlin. I hear now that he has returned to England and is dying—dying, remember, of a broken heart—won't live the year out. He ought to have shot the scoundrel when he had a chance. Not her fault, perhaps—not his fault—fault of a man he trusted—that both trusted, that's the worst of it."

Bayard sat gazing into the fire, its glow deepening the color of his bronze cheek and bringing into high relief a body so strong and well knit that it was difficult to believe that scarcely a year had passed since he dragged himself, starving and half dead, from the depths of an African jungle.

So far he had taken no part in the discussion. Mme. Constantin, who knew his every mood, had seen his face grow grave, his lips straighten, and a certain subdued impatience express itself in the opening and shutting of his hands, but no word of comment had followed.

"Come, we are waiting, Bayard," she said at last, with a smile. "What do you think of Greenough's theory?"

The traveller pushed his cup from him, shook the ashes from his cigar, and answered slowly:—

"That there is something stronger than vengeance, Louise — something higher."

"You mean mercy?"

"Something infinitely more powerful — the Primeval."

The Baron twisted his short neck and faced the speaker. Greenough rose to his feet, relighted his cigar at the silver lamp, and said with some impatience: —

"I don't understand your meaning, Bayard; make it clear, will you?"

"You don't understand, Greenough, because you have not suffered — not as some men I know, not as one man I have in mind."

Mme. Constantin slipped from her cushions, crossed to where Bayard sat, and nestled on a low ottoman beside him.

"Is it something you haven't told me, Bayard?" she asked, looking up into his face. These two had been friends for years. Sometimes in his wanderings the letters came in bunches; at other times the silence continued for months.

"Yes, something I haven't told you, Louise — not all of it. I remember writing you about his arrival at Babohunga, and what a delightful fellow he was, but I couldn't tell you the rest of it. I will now, and I want Greenough to listen."

"He was, I think, the handsomest young fellow that I ever saw—tall, broad shouldered, well built, curly hair cut close to his head, light, upturned mustache, white teeth, clear, fair skin—really you'd hardly meet another such young fellow anywhere. He had come up from Zanzibar and had pushed on to my camp, hoping, he said, to join some caravan going into the interior. He explained that he was an officer in the Belgian army, that he had friends further up, near Lake Mantumba, and that he came for sport alone. I, of course, was glad to take him in— glad that year to take anybody in who was white, especially this young fellow, who was such a contrast to the customary straggler— escaped convict, broken-down gambler, disgraced officer, Arab trader, and other riffraff that occasionally passed my way.

"And then, again, his manners, his smile, the easy grace of his movements—even his linen, bearing his initials and a crown—something he never referred to—all showed him to be a man accustomed to the refinements of society. Another reason was his evident inexperience with the life about him. His ten days' march from the landing below to my camp had been a singularly lucky one. They generally plunge into the forest in perfect health, only to crawl back to the river — those who live to crawl — their bones picked clean by its merciless fingers. To push on now, with the rainy season setting in, meant certain death.

"The second day he paid the price and fell ill. He complained of his feet — the tramp had knocked him out, he said. I examined his toes, cut out some poisonous wood ticks that had buried themselves under the skin, and put him to bed. Fever then set in, and for two days and nights I thought he would go under. During the delirium he kept repeating a woman's name, begging her to give him a drink, to lift his head so he could look into her eyes. Once I had to hold him by main force to keep him from following this fancy of his brain into the forest. When he began to hobble about once more he again wanted to push on, but I determined to hold onto him. I was alone at the time — that is, without a white companion, Judson having gone down to Zanzibar with some despatches for the company — and his companionship was a godsend.

"What seemed to worry him most after he got well was his enforced use of my wardrobe and outfit. He had brought little of his own except his clothes and some blankets, and no arms of any kind but the revolver he carried

187

around his waist in a holster. All his heavier luggage, he explained, was at a landing below. This objection I met by promising to send for it by the first band of carriers after the rainy season was over. In the meantime he must, I insisted, use my own guns and ammunition, or anything else that my kit afforded.

"Up to this time he had never mentioned his home or the names of any of his people, nor had he offered any explanation of his choice of Africa as a hunting ground, nor did he ever seek to learn my own impressions regarding his self-imposed exile (it was really exile, for he never hunted a single day while he was with me), except to ask me one morning in a casual way, whether anything he had said in his delirium had made me think the less of him — all of which I laughed at, never mentioning, of course, what I had been obliged to hear.

"One night, when a tropical storm of unusual severity was passing, I found him sealing a letter at my table with the aid of a lantern held close. Presently he got up and began pacing the floor, seemingly in great agitation; then he reached over, picked up the letter from the table, lighted one end of it in the blaze of the lantern, dropped it to the floor, waited until it was entirely consumed, and then put his foot on the ashes.

"'Rather a waste of time, wasn't it?' I said with a laugh.

"'Yes, all of it has been a waste of time — and my life with it. Now and then I write these letters. They're always burned in the end. No use — nothing to gain. Yes, waste of time. There are some things in the world that no man ought ever to ask forgiveness for.' He threw himself into a chair and went on: —

"'You never went crazy mad over a woman, did you? No — you're not built that way. I am. She was different from the women I had met. She was not of my people — she was English. We met first in Brussels; then I followed her to Vienna. For six months she was free to do as she pleased. We lived the life — well, you know! Then her husband returned.'

"'Oh, she was married!' I remarked casually.

"'Yes, and to a man you would have thought she would have been true to, although he was nearly twice her age. I knew all this — knew when I started in to make her love me — as a matter of pride first — as a boy walks on thin ice, believing he can cross in safety. Perhaps she had some such idea about me. Then the crust gave way, and we were both in the depths. The affair had lasted about six months — all the time her husband was gone. Then I either had to face the consequences or leave Vienna. To have done the first meant ruin to her; the last meant ruin to me. It had not been her fault— it had been mine. He sent me word that he would shoot me at sight, and he meant it. But the madness had not worked out of me yet. She clung to me like a frightened child in her agony, begging me not to leave her — not to meet her husband; to go somewhere—suddenly, as if I had been ordered away by my government; to make no reply to her husband, who, so far, could prove nothing— somewhere, later on, when he was again on a mission, we could meet.

"'You have known me now for some time— the last month intimately. Do I look like a coward and a cur? Well, I am both. That very night I saw him coming toward my quarters in search of me. Did I face him? No. I stooped down behind a fence and hid until he passed.

"'That summer, some months later, we met in Lucerne. She had left him in Venice and he was to meet her in Paris. Two days later he walked into the small hotel where she had stopped and the end came.

"'But I took her with me this time. One of the porters who knew him and knew her helped; and we boarded the night train for Paris without

his finding us. I had then given up about everything in life; I was away without leave, had
lost touch with my world — with everybody —
except my agents, who sent me money. Then
began a still hunt, he following us and we shifting from place to place, until we hid ourselves
in a little town in Northern Italy.

"'Two years had now passed, I still crazy
mad—knowing nothing, thinking nothing—one
blind idolatry! One morning I found a note on
my table; she was going to Venice. I was not
to follow until she sent for me. She never sent
—not a line—no message. Then the truth
came out—she never intended to send—she
was tired of it all!'

"The young fellow rose from his seat and
began pacing the dirt floor again. He seemed
strangely stirred. I waited for the sequel, but
he kept silent.

"'Is this why you came here?' I asked.

"'Yes and no. I came here because one of
my brother officers is at one of the stations up
the river, and because here I could be lost. You
can explain it as you will, but go where I may I
live in deadly fear of meeting the man I wronged.
Here he can't hunt me, as he has done all over
Europe. If we meet there is but one thing left
—either I must kill him or he will kill me. I

would have faced him at any time but for her. Now I could not harm him. We have both suffered from the same cause — the loss of a woman we loved. I had caused his agony and it is for me to make amends, but not by sending him to his grave. Here he is out of my way and I out of his. You saw me burn that letter; I have destroyed dozens of them. When I can stand the pressure no longer I sit down and ask his pardon; then I tear it up or burn it. He couldn't understand — wouldn't understand. He'd think I was afraid to meet him and was begging for my life. Don't you see how impossible it all is — how damnably I am placed?'"

Mme. Constantin and the others had gathered closer to where Bayard sat. Even the wife of the young secretary had moved her chair so she could look into the speaker's face. All were absorbed in the story. Bayard went on:—

"One of the queer things about the African fever is the way it affects the brain. The delirium passes when the temperature goes down, but certain hallucinations last sometimes for weeks. How much of the queer story was true, therefore, and how much was due to his convalescence — he was by no means himself again — I could not decide. That a man should lose his soul and freedom over a woman was not new, but that he should bury himself in the jungle to keep from killing a man whose pardon he wanted to ask for betraying his wife was new.

"I sympathized with him, of course, telling him he was too young to let the world go by; that when the husband got cool he would give up the chase—had given it up long ago, no doubt, now that he realized how good for nothing the woman was—said all the things, of course, one naturally says to a man you suspect to be slightly out of his head.

"The next night Judson returned. He brought newspapers and letters, and word from the outside world; among other things that he had met a man at the landing below who was on his way to the camp above us. He had offered to bring him with him, but he had engaged some Zanzibari of his own and intended to make a shorter route to the north of our camp and then join one of the bands in charge of an Arab trader—some of Tippu-Tib's men really. He knew of the imminence of the rainy season and wanted to return to Zanzibar before it set in in earnest. Judson's news—all his happenings, for that matter—interested the young Belgian even more than they did me, and before the week was out the two were constantly together—a godsend in his present state of mind—saved him in fact from a relapse, I thought—Judson's odd way of looking at things, as well as his hard, common sense, being just what the high-strung young fellow needed most.

"Some weeks after this—perhaps two, I can't remember exactly — a party of my men whom I sent out for plantains and corn (our provisions were running low) returned to camp bringing me a scrap of paper which a white man had given them. They had found him half dead a day's journey away. On it was scrawled in French a request for food and help. I started at once, taking the things I knew would be wanted. The young Belgian offered to go with me — he was always ready to help — but Judson had gone to a neighboring village and there was no one to leave in charge but him. I had now not only begun to like him but to trust him.

"I have seen a good many starving men in my time, but this lost stranger when I found him was the most miserable object I ever beheld. He lay propped up against a tree, with his feet over a pool of water, near where my men had left him. His eyes were sunk in his head, his lips parched and cracked, his voice almost gone. A few hours more and he would have been beyond help. He had fainted, so they told me, after writing the scrawl, and only the efforts of my men and the morsel of food they could spare him brought him back to life. When I had poured a few drops of brandy down his throat and had made him a broth and warmed him up his strength began to come back. It is astonishing what a few ounces of food will do for a starving man.

"He told me he had been deserted by his carriers, who had robbed him of all he had — food, ammunition, everything — and since then he had wandered aimlessly about, living on bitter berries and fungi. He had, it appears, been sent to Zanzibar by his government to straighten out some matters connected with one of the missions, and, wishing to see something of the country, he had pushed on, relying on his former experiences — he had been on similar excursions in Brazil — to pull him through.

"Then followed the story of the last few weeks — the terrors of the long nights, as he listened to the cries of prowling animals; his hunger and increasing weakness — the counting of the days and hours he could live; the indescribable fright that overpowered him when he realized he must die, alone, and away from his people. Raising himself on his elbow — he was still too weak to stand on his feet — he motioned to me to come nearer, and, as I bent my head he said in a hoarse whisper, as if he were in the presence of some mighty spirit who would over-hear: —

"'In these awful weeks I have faced the primeval. God stripped me naked—naked as Adam, and like him, left me alone. In my hunger I cried out; in my weakness I prayed. No answer—nothing but silence — horrible, over-powering silence. Then in my despair I began to curse—to strike the trees with my clenched fists, only to sink down exhausted. I could not—I would not die! Soon all my life passed in review. All the mean things I had done to others; all the mean things they had done to me. Then love, honor, hatred, revenge, offi-cial promotion, money, the good opinion of my fellows—all the things we value and that make our standards — took form, one after another, and as quickly vanished in the gloom of the jungle. Of what use were they —any of them? If I was to live I must again become the Homo—the Primeval Man—eat as he ate, sleep as he slept, be simple, brave, forgiving, obedient, as he had been. All I had brought with me of civilization—my civilization—the one we men make and call life—were as nothing, if it could not bring me a cup of water, a handful of corn or a coal of fire to warm my shivering body.'

"I am not giving you his exact words, Louise, not all of them, but I am giving you as near as I can the effect untamed, mighty, irresistible nature produced on his mind. Lying there, his shrivelled white face supported on one shrunken hand, his body emaciated so that the bones of his knees and elbows protruded from his ragged clothes, he seemed like some prophet of old, lifting his voice in the wilderness, proclaiming a new faith and a new life.

"Nor can I give you any idea of the way the words came, nor of the glassy brilliance of his eyes, set in a face dry as a skull, the yellow teeth chattering between tightly stretched lips. Oh! it was horrible — horrible!

"The second day he was strong enough to stand, but not to walk. The rain, due now every hour, comes without warning, making the swamps impassable, and there was no time to lose. I left two men to care for him, and hurried back to camp to get some sort of a stretcher on which to bring him out.

"That night, sitting under our lamp—we were alone at the time, my men being again away—I gave the young Belgian the details of my trip, telling him the man's name and object

197

in coming into the wilderness, describing his sufferings and relating scraps of his talk. He listened with a curious expression on his face, his eyes growing strangely bright, his fingers twitching like those of a nervous person unused to tales of suffering and privation.

" ' And he will live?' he said, with a smile, as I finished.

" ' Certainly; all he wanted was something in his stomach; he's got that. He'll be here to-morrow.'

" For some time he did not speak; then he rose from his seat, looked at me steadily for a moment, grasped my hand, and with a certain tenderness in his voice, said:

" ' Thank you.'

" ' For what?' I asked in surprise.

" ' For being kind. I'll go to the spring and get a drink, and then I'll go to sleep. Good night!'

" I watched him disappear into the dark, wondering at his mood. Hardly had I regained my seat when a pistol shot rang out. He had blown the top of his head off.

" That night I buried him in the soft ooze near the spring, covering him so the hyenas could not reach his body.

" The next morning my men arrived, carrying

198

the stranger. He had been plucky and had insisted on walking a little, and the party arrived earlier than I expected. When he had thanked me for what I had done, he began an inspection of my rude dwelling and the smaller lean-to, even peering into the huts connected with my bungalow — new in his experience.

" 'And you are all alone except for your black men?' he asked in an eager tone.

" 'No, I have Mr. Judson with me. He is away this week — and a young Belgian officer — and — I —'

" 'Yes, I remember Mr. Judson,' he interrupted. 'I met him at the landing below. I should have taken his advice and joined him. And the young officer — has he been long with you?'

" 'About two months.'

" 'He is the same man who left some of his luggage at the landing below, is he not?'

" 'Yes, I think so,' I answered.

" 'A young man with light curly hair and upturned mustache, very strong, quick in his movements, shows his teeth when he speaks — very white teeth —'

" He was smiling — a strange smile from one whose lips were still parched.

" 'Yes,' I replied.

"'Can I see him?'

"'No, he is dead!'

"Had I not stretched out my hand to steady him he would have fallen.

"'Dead!' he cried, a look of horror in his eyes. 'No! You don't mean—not starved to death! No, no, you don't mean that!' He was trembling all over.

"'No, he blew out his brains last night. His grave is outside. Come, I will show it to you.'

"I had almost to carry him. For an instant he leaned against a tree growing near the poor fellow's head, his eyes fixed on the rude mound. Then he slowly sank to his knees and burst into tears, sobbing:

"'Oh! If I could have stopped him! He was so young to die.'

"Two days later he set out on his return to the coast."

With the ending of the story, Bayard turned to Mme. Constantin:

"There, Louise, you have the rest of it. You understand now what I meant when I said there was something stronger than revenge;—the primeval."

Greenough, who had sat absorbed, drinking in every word, laid his hand on Bayard's shoulder.

" You haven't told us their names."

"Do you want them?"

"Yes, but write them on this card."

Bayard slipped his gold pencil from its chain and traced two names.

" My God, Bayard!   That's the same man I told you is dying of a broken heart."

"Yes—that's why I told you the story, Greenough.   But his heart is not breaking for the woman he loved and lost, but for the man he hunted— the man I buried."

THE PARTHENON BY WAY OF PAPEN-
DRECHT

"WILYUM! . . . . . *Wilyum!* . . . . .
WILYUM!"

It was mine host of the Ferry Inn at Cookham who was calling, and at the top of his
voice — and a big-chested voice it was — the
sound leaping into crescendo as the object of his
search remained hidden. Then he turned to
me:

"He's somewheres 'round the boat house —
you can't miss him — there's too much of him!"

"Are ye wantin' me, sor?" came another
shout as I rounded the squat building stuffed
with boats — literally so — bottom, top, and
sides.

"Yes — are you the boatman?"

"I am, sor — and bloody sick of me job. Do
ye see that wherry shovin' off — the one with
the lady in a sweater? Yes — that's right —
just slipped under the bridge. Well, sor, what
d'ye think the bloke did for me? Look at it,
sor!" (Here he held out his hand, in which
lay a half-penny.) "And me a-washin' out 'is

202

boat, feedin' of 'is dog, and keepin' an eye on 'is togs and 'is ladies — and then shoves off and 'ands me this — a 'a'penny, sor — *a 'a' penny* — from the likes o' 'im to the likes o' me! Damn 'im!'"— and away went the coin into the river. "You'll excuse me, sor, but I couldn't choke it down. Is it a punt ye're lookin' for?"

The landlord was right — there was a good deal of him — six feet and an inch, I should think; straight as an oar, his bared arms swinging free; waist, thighs, and back tough as a saw-log. To this was added two big blue eyes set in a clean-shaven face bronzed by the sun, and a double row of teeth that would have shamed an ear of corn. I caught, too, the muscles of his chest rounding out his boating shirt, and particularly the muscles of the neck supporting the round head crowned with closely cropped hair — evidently a young Englishman of that great middle class which the nation depends upon in an emergency. My inspection also settled any question I might have had as to why he was "William," and never "Bill," to those about him.

The one thing lacking in his make-up — and which only came into view when he turned his head — was the upper part of one ear. This was clipped as close as a terrier's.

Again he repeated the question — with a deprecatory smile, as if he already regretted his outburst.

"Is it a punt ye're wantin', sor?"

"Yes — and a man to pole it and look after me while I paint. I had old Norris for the past few years, but I hear he's gone back to gardening. Will you have time with your other work?"

"Time! I'll chuck my job if I don't."

"No, — you can do both, — Norris did. You can pole me out to where I want to work; bring me my lunch when you have yours, and come for me at night. You weren't here two years ago — were you?"

"No — I was with General French. Got this clip outside Kimberly—" and he touched his ear. "Been all my life on the river — Maidenhead and Bourne's End mostly — and so when my time was up I come home and the boss here put me on."

"A soldier! I thought so. I see now why you got mad. Wonder you didn't throw that chap into the river." I am a crank on the happiness one gets from the giving of tips — and a half-penny man is the rock bottom of meanness.

His face straightened.

"Well, we can't do that, sor — we can't

never talk back. Got to grin and bear it or lose yer job. Learned that in the Hussahs. I didn't care for his money — maybe it was the way he did it that set me goin' — as if I was — Well — let it go! And it's a punt ye want? — Yes, sor — come and pick it out."

After that it was plain sailing — or punting. The picture of that London cad sprawling in the water, which my approval had created in his mind, had done it. And it was early and late too (there were few visitors that month) ; down by the Weir below the lock as far as Cliveden ; up the backwater to the Mill — William stretched beside me while I worked, or pulling back and forth when a cool bottle — beer, of course — or a kettle and an alcohol lamp would add to my comfort.

Many years of tramping and boating up and down the Thames from Reading to Maidenhead have taught me the ins and outs of the river. I know it as I do my own pocket (and there is more in that statement than you think — especially during regatta week).

First comes Sonning with its rose gardens and quaint brick bridge ; and then Marlowe with that long stretch of silver bordered by nodding trees and dominated by the robber Inn — four shillings

and six for a sawdust sandwich! Then Maidenhead, swarming with boats and city folks after
dark (it is only a step from the landing to any
number of curtained sitting-rooms with shaded
candles — and there be gay times at Maidenhead,
let me tell you!). And, between, best of all,
lovely Cookham.

Here the river, crazy with delight, seems to lose
its head and goes meandering about, poking its
nose up backwaters, creeping across meadows,
flooding limpid shallows, mirroring oaks and
willows upside down, surging up as if to sweep
away a velvet-shorn lawn, only to pour itself —
its united self — into an open-mouthed lock, and
so on to a saner life in a level stretch beyond.
If you want a map giving these vagaries, spill a
cup of tea and follow its big and little puddles
with their connecting rivulets : ten chances to
one it will come out right.

All this William and I took in for three un-
broken weeks, my usual summer allotment on
the Thames. Never was there such a breezy,
wholesome companion; stories of his life in the
Veldt; of his hospital experience over that same
ear — " The only crack I got, sor, thank God ! —
except bein' 'alf starved for a week and down
two months with the fever —" neither of which
seemed to have caused him a moment's incon-

206

venience; stories of the people living about him and those who came from London with a "'am sandwidge in a noospaper, and precious little more," rolled out of him by the hour.

And the poise of the man! When he lay stretched out beside me on the grass while I worked—an old bivouac attitude—he kept still; no twitching of legs or stretching of arms —lay as a big hound does, whose blood and breeding necessitate repose.

And we were never separated. First a plunge overboard, and then a pull back for breakfast, and off again with the luncheon tucked under the seat—and so on until the sun dropped behind the hills.

The only days on which this routine of work and play had to be changed were Sundays and holidays. Then my white umbrella would loom up as large as a circus tent, the usual crowd surging about its doors. As you cannot see London for the people, so you cannot see the river for boats on these days—all sorts of boats —wherries, tubs, launches, racing crafts, shells, punts—everything that can be poled, pulled, or wobbled, and in each one the invariable combination—a man, a girl, and a dog—a dog, a girl, and a man. This has been going on for ages, and will to the end of time.

On these mornings William and I have our bath early—ahead of the crowd really, who generally arrive two hours after sunrise and keep up the pace until the last train leaves for Paddington. This bath is at the end of one of the teacup spillways, and is called the Weir. There is a plateau, a plunge down some twenty feet into a deep pool, and the usual surroundings of fresh morning air, gay tree-tops, and the splash of cool water sparkling in the sunlight.

To-day as my boat grated on the gravel my eyes fell on a young English lord who was holding the centre of the stage in the sunlight. He was dressed from head to foot in a skin-tight suit of underwear which had been cut for him by a Garden-of-Eden tailor. He was just out of the water—a straight, well-built, ruddy-skinned fellow—every inch a man! What birth and station had done for him would become apparent when his valet began to hand him his Bond Street outfit. The next instant William stood beside him. Then there came a wriggle about the shoulders, the slip of a buckle, and he was overboard and out again before my lord had discarded his third towel.

I fell to thinking.

Naked they were equals. That was the way they came into the world and that's the way they would go out. And yet within the hour my lord would be back to his muffins and silver service, with two flunkies behind his chair, and William would be swabbing out a boat or poling me home through the pond lilies.

But why?—I kept asking myself. A totally idiotic and illogical question, of course. Both were of an age; both would be a joy to a sculptor looking for modern gods with which to imitate the Greek ones. Both were equal in the sight of their Maker. Both had served their country—my lord, I learned later, being one of the first to draw a bead on Spion Kop close enough to be of any use—and both were honest—at least William was—and the lord must have been.

There is no answer—never can be. And yet the picture of the two as they stood glistening in the sunlight continues to rise in my memory, and with it always comes this same query—one which will never down—Why should there be the difference?

But the summer is moving on apace. There is another Inn and another William—or rather, there was one several hundred years ago before he went off crusading. It is an old resort of mine. Seven years now has old Leah filled my breakfast cup with a coffee that deserves a hymn of praise in its honor. I like it hot — boiling, blistering hot, and the old woman brings it on the run, her white sabots clattering across the flower-smothered courtyard. During all these years I have followed with reverent fingers not only the slopes of its roof but the loops of swinging clematis that crowd its balconies and gables as well. I say "my" because I have known this Inn of William the Conqueror long enough to include it in the list of the many good ones I frequent over Europe — the Bellevue, for instance, at Dordrecht, over against Papendrecht (I shall be there in another month). And the Britannia in Venice, and I hope still a third in unknown Athens — unknown to me — my objective point this year.

This particular Inn with the roof and the clematis, is at Dives, twenty miles from Trouville on the coast. You never saw anything like it, and you never will again. I hold no brief for my old friend Le Remois, the proprietor, but the coffee is not the only thing over which grateful men chant hymns. There is a kitchen, resplendent in polished brass, with three French chefs in attendance, and a two-century-old spit for roasting. There is the wine-cellar, in which cobwebs and not labels record the age and the vintage; there is a dining-room — three of them — with baronial fireplaces, sixteenth-century furniture, and linen and glass to match — to say nothing of tapestries, Spanish leathers, shrines, carved saints, ivories, and pewter — the whole a sight to turn bric-a-brac fiends into burglars—not a difficult thing by the way — and then, of course — there is the bill!

"Where have you been, M. Le Remois?" asked a charming woman.

"To church, Madame."

"Did you say your prayers?"

"Yes, Madame," answered this good boniface, with a twinkle.

"What did you pray for?"

"I said — 'Oh, Lord! — do not make me rich, but place me *next* to the rich'" — and he kept on his way rubbing his hands and chuckling. And yet I must say it is worth the price.

I have no need of a William here — nor of anybody else. The water for my cups is within my reach; convenient umbrellas on movable pedestals can be shoved into place; a sheltered back porch hives for the night all my paraphernalia and unfinished sketches, and a step or two brings me to a table where a broiled lobster fresh from the sea and a peculiar peach ablaze in a peculiar sauce — the whole washed down by a pint of —

(No — you can't have the brand — there were only seven bottles left when I paid my bill) — and besides I am going back — help to ease the cares that beset a painter's life.

But even this oasis of a garden, hemmed about as if by the froth of Trouville and the suds of Cabourg; through which floats the gay life of Paris resplendent in toilets never excelled or *exceeded* anywhere — cannot keep me from Holland very long. And it is a pity too, for of late years I have been looked upon as a harmless fixture at the Inn — so much so that men and women pass and repass my easel, or look over my shoulder while I work without a break in their confidences — quite as if I was a deaf, dumb, and blind waiter, or twin-brother to old Coco the cockatoo, who has surveyed the same scene from his perch near the roof for the past thirty years.

None of these unconscious ear-droppings am I going to betray — delightful, startling—*improper*, if you must have it—as some of them were. Not the most interesting, at all events, for I promised her I wouldn't — but there is no question as to the diversion obtained by keeping the latch-string of your ears on the outside.

None of all this ever drips into my auricles in Holland. A country so small that they build dikes to keep the inhabitants from being spilt off the edge, is hardly the place for a scandal — certainly not in stolid Dordrecht or in that fly-speck of a Papendrecht, whose dormer windows peer over the edge of the dike as if in mortal fear of another inundation. And yet, small as it is, it is still big enough for me to approach it — the fly-speck, of course — by half a dozen different routes. I can come by boat from Rotterdam. Fop Smit owns and runs it — (no kin of mine, more's the pity) — or by train from Amsterdam; or by carriage from any number of 'dams, 'drechts, and 'bergs. Or I can tramp it on foot, or be wheeled in on a dog-wagon. I have tried them all, and know. Being now a staid old painter and past such fool-ishness, I take the train.

Toot! Toot! — and I am out on the platform, through the door of the station and aboard the one-horse tram that wiggles and swings over the cobble-scoured streets of Dordrecht, and so on to the Bellevue.

Why I stop at the Bellevue (apart from it being one of my Inns) is that from its windows I can-not only watch the life of the tawny-colored, boat-crowded Maas, but see every curl of smoke that mounts from the chimneys of Papendrecht strung along its opposite bank. My dear friend,

Herr Boudier, of years gone by, has retired from its ownership, but his successor, Herr Teitsma, is as hearty in his welcome. Peter, my old boatman, too, pulled his last oar some two years back, and one "Bop" takes his place. There is another "p" and an "e" tacked on to Bop, but I have eliminated the unnecessary and call him "Bob" for short. They made Bob out of what was left of Peter, but they left out all trace of William.

This wooden-shod curiosity is anywhere from seventy to one hundred and fifty years old, gray, knock-kneed, bent in the back, and goes to sleep standing up — *and stays asleep*. He is the exact duplicate of the tramp in the comic opera of "Miss Hook of Holland" — except that the actor-sleeper occasionally topples over and has to be braced up. Bob is past-master of the art and goes it alone, without propping of any kind. He is the only man in Dordrecht, or Papendrecht, or the country round about, who can pull a boat and speak English. He says so, and I am forced not only to believe him, but to hire him. He wants it in advance, too — having had some experience with "painter-man," he explains to Herr Teitsma.

I shall, of course, miss my delightful William, but I am accustomed to that. And, then, again,

THE OLD GROOTE KIRK, DORDRECHT.

while Bob asleep is an interesting physiological study, Bob awake adds to the gayety of nations, samples of which crowd about my easel, Holland being one of the main highways of the earth.

I have known Dort and the little 'drecht across the way for some fifteen years, five of which have slipped by since I last opened my umbrella along its quaint quays. To my great joy nothing has changed. The old potato boat still lies close to the quay, under the overhanging elms. The same dear old man and his equally dear old wife still make their home beneath its hipped roof. I know, for it is here I lunch, the cargo forming the chief dish, followed by a saucer of stewed currants, a cup of coffee — (more hymns here) — and a loaf of bread from the baker's. The old Groote Kirk still towers aloft — the highest building in Holland, they say; the lazy, red-sailed luggers drift up and down, their decks gay with potted plants; swiss curtains at the cabin windows, the wife holding the tiller while the man trims the sail. The boys still clatter over the polished cobbles — an aggressive mob when school lets out—and a larger crop, I think, than in the years gone by, and with more noise — my umbrella being the target. Often a spoilt fish or half a last week's cabbage comes my way, whereupon Bob awakes to instant action

215

with a consequent scattering, the bravest and most agile making faces from behind wharf spiles and corners. Peter used to build a fence of oars around me to keep them off, but Bob takes it out in swearing.

Only once did he silence them. They were full grown, this squad, and had crowded the old man against a tree under which I had backed as shelter from a passing shower. There came a blow straight from the shoulder, a sprawling boy, and Bob was in the midst of them, his right sleeve rolled up, showing a full-rigged ship tattooed in India ink. What poured from him I learned afterward was an account of his many voyages to the Arctic and around the Horn, as the label on his arm proved—an experience which, he shouted, would be utilized in pounding them up into fish bait if they did not take to their heels. After that he always went to sleep with one eye open, the boys keeping awake with two—and out of my way—a result which interested me the more.

If my Luigi was not growing restless in my beloved Venice (it is wonderful how large a portion of the earth I own) I would love to pass the rest of my summer along these gray canals, especially since Bob's development brings a daily surprise. Only to-day I caught sight of him

216

half hidden in an angle of a wall, surrounded by a group of little tots who were begging him for paper pin-wheels which a vender had stopped to sell, an infinitesimal small coin the size of a cuff button purchasing a dozen or more. When I again looked up from a canvas each tot had a pin-wheel, and later on Bob, that much poorer in pocket, sneaked back and promptly went to sleep.

But even Bob's future beatification cannot hold me. I yearn for the white, blinding light and breathless lagoons, and all that makes Venice the Queen City of the World.

Luigi meets me *inside* the station. It takes a *soldo* to get in, and Luigi has but few of them, but he is always there. His gondola is moored to the landing steps outside—a black swan of a boat, all morocco cushions and silk fringes; the product of a thousand years of tinkering by the most fastidious and luxurious people of ancient or modern times, and still to-day the most comfortable conveyance known to man.

Hurry up, you who have never known a gondola or a Luigi! A vile-smelling, chuggity-chug is forcing its way up every crooked canal, no matter how narrow. Two Venetian ship-yards are hammering away on their hulls or polishing their motors. Soon the cost of pro-

217

duction will drop to that of a gondola. Then
look out! Theré are eight thousand machinists
in the Arsenal earning but five francs a day, any
one of whom can learn to run a motor boat in a
week, thus doubling their wages. Worse yet—
the world is getting keener every hour for speedy
things. I may be wrong—I hope and pray I
am—but it seems to me that the handwriting is
already on the wall. "This way to the Museo
Civico," it reads—"if you want to find a gondola of twenty-five years ago." As for the
Luigis and the Esperos—they will then have
given up the unequal struggle.

The only hope rests with the Venetians themselves. They have restored the scarred Library,
and are rebuilding the Campanile, with a reverence for the things which made their past
glorious that commands the respect of the artis-
tic world. The gondola is as much a part of
Venice as its sunsets, pigeons, and palaces. Let
them by special license keep the Traghetti intact,
with their shuttles of gondolas crossing back and
forth — then, perhaps, the catastrophe may be
deferred for a few decades.

As it was in Dort and Papendrecht so it is in
Venice. Except these beastly, vile-smelling
boats there is nothing new, thank God. Every-

thing else is faded, weather-worn, and old, everything filled with sensuous beauty—sky, earth, lagoon, garden wall, murmuring ripples — the same wonderful Venice that thrills its lovers the world over.

And the old painters are still here—Walter Brown, Bunce, Bompard, Faulkner, and the rest —successors of Ziem and Rico—men who have loved her all their lives. And with them a new band of devotees—Monet and Louis Aston Knight among them. "For a few days," they said in explanation, but it was weeks before they left—only to return, I predict, as long as they can hold a brush.

As for Luigi and me—we keep on our accustomed way, leading our accustomed lives. Seventeen years now since he bent to his oar behind my cushions—twenty-six in all since I began to idle about her canals. It is either the little canal next the Public Garden, or up the Giudecca, or under the bronze horses of San Marco; or it may be we are camped out in the Piazzetta before the Porta della Carta; or perhaps up the narrow canal of San Rocco, or in the Fruit Market near the Rialto while the boats unload their cargoes.

All old subjects and yet ever new; each has been painted a thousand times, and in as many different lights and perspectives. And yet each canvas differs from its fellows as do two ripples or two morning skies.

For weeks we drift about. One day Carlotta, the fishwife up the Fondamenta della Pallada, makes us our coffee; the next Luigi buys it of some smart café on the Piazza. This with a roll, a bit of Gorgonzola, and a bunch of grapes, or half a dozen figs, is our luncheon, to which is added two curls of blue smoke, one from Luigi's pipe and the other from my cigarette. Then we fall to work again.

But this will never do! While I have been loafing with Luigi not only has the summer slipped away, but the cool winds of October have crept down from the Alps. There are fresh subjects to tackle—some I have never seen. Athens beckons to me. The columns of the Parthenon loom up!

If there are half a dozen ways of getting into Papendrecht—there is only one of reaching Athens—that is, if you start from Venice. Trieste first, either by rail or boat, and then aboard one of the Austrian Lloyds, and so on down the Adriatic to Patras.

It is October, remember—when every spear of grass from a six months' drought—the cus-

SAN MARCO FROM THE MERCERIA, VENICE.

tomary dry spell—is burnt to a crisp. It will rain to-morrow, or next week, they will tell you —but it doesn't—never has in October—and never will. Strange to say, you never miss it —neither in the color of the mountains flanking the Adriatic or in any of the ports on the way down, or in Patras itself. The green note to which I have been accustomed—which I have labored over all my life—is lacking, and a new palette takes its place—of mauve, violet, indescribable blues, and evanescent soap-bubble reds. The slopes of the hills are mother-of-pearl, their tops melting into cloud shadows so delicate in tone that you cannot distinguish where one leaves off and the other begins.

And it is so in Patras, except for a riotous, defiant pine — green as a spring cabbage or a newly painted shutter — that sucks its moisture from nobody knows where — hasn't any, perhaps, and glories in its shame. All along the railroad from the harbor of Patras to the outskirts of Athens it is the same — bare fields, bare hills, streets and roads choked with dust. And so, too, when you arrive at the station and take the omnibus for the Grand Bretagne.

By this time you are accustomed to it — in fact you rather enjoy it. If you have a doubt of it, step out on the balcony at the front of the hotel and look up!

Hanging in the sky — in an air of pure ether, set in films of silver grays in which shimmer millions of tones, delicate as the shadings of a pearl, towers the Acropolis, its crest fringed by the ruins of the greatest temples the world possesses.

I rang a bell.

"Get me a carriage and send me up a guide — anybody who can speak English and who is big enough to carry a sketch trap."

He must have been outside, so quickly did he answer the call. He was two-thirds the size of William, one-half the length of Luigi, and one-third the age of Bob.

"What is your name?"

"Vlassopoulos."

"Anything else?"

"Yes—Panis."

"Then we'll drop the last half. Put those traps in the carriage — and take me to the Parthenon."

I never left it for fourteen consecutive days — nor did I see a square inch of Athens other than the streets I drove through up and back on my way to work. Nor have I in all my experience ever had a more competent, obliging, and companionable guide — always excepting my beloved Luigi, who is not only my guide, but my protector and friend as well.

It was then that I blessed the dust. Green things, wet things, soggy things — such as mud and dull skies — have no place in the scheme of the Parthenon and its contiguous temples and ruins. That wonderful tea-rose marble, with its stains of burnt sienna marking the flutings of endless broken columns, needs no varnishing of moisture to enhance its beauty. That will do for the façade of Burlington House with its grimy gray statues, or the moss-encrusted tower of the Groote Kirk, but never here. It was this fear, perhaps, that kept me at work, haunted as I was by the bogy of "Rain to-morrow. It always comes, and keeps on for a month when it starts in." Blessed be the weather clerk! It never started in — not until I reached Brindisi on my way back to Paris; then, if I remember, there was some falling weather — at the rate of two inches an hour.

And yet I might as well confess that my fourteen days of consecutive study of the Acropolis, beginning at the recently uncovered entrance gate and ending in the Museum behind the Parthenon, added nothing to my previous historical or other knowledge — meagre as it had been.

Where the Venetians wrought the greatest havoc, how many and what columns were thrown down ; how high and thick and massive they were; what parts of the marvellous ruin that High Robber Chief Lord Elgin stole and carted off to London, and still keeps the British Museum acting as "fence"; how wide and long and spacious was the superb chamber that held the statue the gods loved — none of these things interested me — do not now. What I saw was an epoch in stone; a chronicle telling the story of civilization; a glove thrown down to posterity, challenging the competition of the world.

And with this came a feeling of reverence so profound, so awe-inspiring, so humbling, that I caught myself speaking to Panis in whispers — as one does in a temple when the service is in progress. This, as the sun sped its course and the purple shadows of the coming night began to creep up the steps and columns of the marvellous pile, its pediment bathed in the rose-glow of the fading day, was followed by a silence that neither of us cared to break. For then the wondrous temple took on the semblance of some old sage, the sunlight on his forehead, the shadow of the future about his knees.

224

Date Due